D1552799

FIELDS' GUIDE TO ASSASSINS

JULIE MULHERN

J & M PRESS

ISBN - 97-81723813047

❀ Created with Vellum

FOR MY FAMILY

ACKNOWLEDGMENTS

THANK YOU TO GRETCHEN AND RACHEL, WHO MADE THIS BOOK BETTER.

THANK YOU TO MATT, FOR KEEPING THE FAITH.

THANK YOU TO MER AND KATIE, FOR BEING YOU.

ONE

"People are staring," I muttered.

My friend André DuChamp favored me with a good-natured grin. "Of course they're staring. You're like the most famous person on the planet."

The moment I'd stepped out of the limousine onto the rain-slicked Parisian sidewalk, I'd felt hundreds of eyes sizing me up—judging everything from my hair and makeup to my shoes. The *click-click-click* of cameras didn't help with the under-a-microscope feeling that had dogged me since my return from Mexico.

All those cameras—all those watching eyes—weren't helping my nerves. Not one bit. I needed a moment to collect myself—this was my first assignment and I couldn't screw it up.

There were no quiet moments to be had—not with the swarm of photographers and André's hand tugging at my elbow.

I swallowed. Hard. Then tilted my head to look at our destination.

The club's entrance looked exactly like the Arc de Triomphe. Already the line to get inside snaked around the block.

André had insisted on this place and, because the man I was supposed to meet was a regular, I hadn't argued.

"C'mon." André ushered me—ushered us (I was so annoyed about us)—to the club's door, where a muscle-bound bouncer wearing a black T-shirt and jacket unhooked the clip from the stanchion.

I hated jumping lines. I dug my heels into the pavement and looked at the hundreds of people waiting to get in. "I always feel weird doing this."

"Poppy—" with an indulgent shake of his head, André dismissed my egalitarian leanings "—these people are waiting because Triomphe is happening. Your being here makes it happening."

Escaping from a Mexican drug lord does wonders for a girl's Q score. I trended for days. Was still trending. Went from having tens of thousands of Instagram followers to millions. Overnight.

"I'd love to be you," said Dylan Roberts, the reality starlet André had brought along (the annoying part of us). She hooked her arm through mine and flashed smile after smile at the photographers. Photographers who were calling my name. *Over here, Poppy! Smile, Poppy! Who are you wearing, Poppy?*

With Dylan focused on the photographers, I gave André a look. André agented reality stars eager to make a quick million or two off their few minutes of fame and Dylan Roberts' star was fading. Having her seen with me would extend her shelf life. He'd used me.

"You love this." He grinned.

I blinked—half blinded by a flash. "No. I don't. I don't even like it."

Dylan shifted her focus from the pack of rabid photographers to me. "How can you not love this? It's the best." Like most reality stars, Dylan was naturally pretty. The right makeup made her beautiful. "You're so lucky." Now she flashed her smile—one perfected by orthodontia and some serious teeth whitening—at me. "You don't have to work at being famous."

Lucky? Dylan and I had very different definitions of lucky. My spine stiffened.

Perhaps André sensed I was about to tell his client where she could put the heels of her Jimmy Choos—maybe even help her put them there. He put his hand on Dylan's back and propelled her forward. "Let's go."

The club's interior was black—black velvet couches, black leather banquettes, and LED lighting in shades of lime and lavender.

"Ooooh." Dylan's lips formed a perfect circle.

"Triomphe is the coolest club in Paris." In Andre's business, he had to know things like that.

"I heard the coolest club in Paris was under a bridge." I was being contrary. But I'd also really heard that.

André sniffed. "The place under the bridge doesn't have VIP seating."

The club was packed. They didn't need more publicity. "How much are they paying you for bringing me here?"

Wherever I went, whatever I did, there were pictures. And commentary. And video. Someone with a cellphone was probably filming right now. Tomorrow—an hour from now—this club would be all over the internet, the line outside would grow exponentially, and André would be paid. Handsomely.

"Be nice." He reached out and squeezed my hand. "I'll take you to Hermés tomorrow."

Really? They must be paying him a fortune. "I've had my eye on a bag—a Toolbox Twenty-Six in bleu atoll."

"I was thinking a scarf."

"Yeah, no." I looked around the packed club and didn't see the man I was supposed to meet. Please let him be here. I didn't want to come back. "This appearance is going to cost you a handbag."

Dylan followed our exchange with a slight furrow between her threaded brows. "Wait. You're not getting paid?"

"No." I was here at the behest of my new boss, but I wasn't about to tell her that. Or André—not when I had him on the line for a Hermés bag.

"You could totally make a ton of money," she insisted.

I simply shrugged.

"I mean it. You're like the most famous person ever." Her voice was wistful.

Being a movie star's daughter (especially when that movie star was Chariss Carlton, the brightest star there was) might have made me famous, but the accident of my birth wasn't exactly an accomplishment. Being abducted by the biggest, baddest, most powerful drug lord in the world wasn't an accomplishment either. Getting away had been. I was famous for all three.

We settled at our table and I scanned the VIP section. He was walking toward us. Ghislain Lambert. The reason I'd agreed to come to this club. He made his way to a table near ours and leaned back against the banquette. My nerves, which had calmed at the mention of Hermés, got up and did the can-can. Could I do this? I swallowed hard. I could do this.

I'd googled him before I came. Ghislain Lambert was the son of a textile merchant who'd married the only daughter of an impecunious count. Lambert had used his aristocratic grandfather's name and threadbare connections to establish himself in business. The man looked like Romain Duris— same great hair, same stubble, same sexy grin. I let my gaze linger long enough to catch his attention. Then I looked away.

The DJ was playing something with a relentless beat and the lights flashed and pulsed. "Dance with me?" I asked André.

He leaned forward. "What?"

I raised my voice. "Dance with me!"

André settled his gaze on Dylan. "Do you mind?"

"Of course not. I'll order drinks." She leaned back against the black leather of the half-circle banquette as if she were sitting on a throne and the people who hadn't made it into the VIP section were her subjects.

André led me onto the dance floor, pausing only to breathe into my ear, "What's up? You never dance."

Blame that on a singularly unflattering picture that almost broke the internet. Wide angle lens plus stripes across my ass plus bending over from the waist for a fallen earring. Lesson learned.

"Nothing's up." Such a lie.

"Yeah, right." André looked around the club—searching. "Who's the guy?"

"I don't know what you mean." I put my hands on his shoulders and swayed my hips.

"Anyone ever told you that you're a terrible liar?"

"Once or twice." Or a million times.

"So who is he?" André was still searching.

"I'll tell you later." I shimmied and prayed no one with a camera was shooting me from behind.

André smirked. "About that handbag…"

"What about it?" I danced closer to him.

"It's yours if you take a couple of selfies with Dylan."

When he sent me to Paris, John Brown, my new boss and the director of a super-secret government agency, had told me, "Convince people there's nothing but air between your ears. Get close to Ghislain Lambert. Learn as much as you can." As to what I was supposed to learn from a private banker to Europe's rich and famous, Mr. Brown hadn't told me that. "Get close to him. Listen."

As directives went, Mr. Brown's was vague.

I leaned forward and spoke over the relentless beat into André's ear. "The handbag *and* a couple of scarves."

"You don't wear scarves."

As if that mattered. "We could do two handbags," I countered.

"You drive a hard bargain."

I merely smiled. And swayed.

"The bag and two scarves?" André was smart to clarify an exact number.

"Not the carrés," I clarified. "I want the shawls. The big ones."

"Poppy." He made my name a complaint.

"Take it or leave it." I snuck a quick peek at Ghislain Lambert. The man was squinting at his phone.

Damn.

I shimmied harder.

The song ended and André led me back to the table, where a waiter was opening a bottle of Champagne.

André read the label on the bottle and blanched. "That's Krug Clos du Mesnil."

I snickered. This would be the last time André ever let Dylan order drinks.

"Dylan—" I grinned at André's client "—you have excellent taste."

She blinked. "I do?"

I nodded. The grapes for the wine she'd ordered came from a tiny walled vineyard in Mesnil-sur-Oger. A bottle cost more than a thousand dollars. "That's very good Champagne."

She shrugged. "I didn't order it. That man over there sent it." She inclined her head toward someone behind me. "I ordered a lemon-drop martini."

André breathed a loud sigh of relief.

I glanced over my shoulder. Ghislain Lambert wasn't squinting at his phone anymore. I nodded an acknowledgment, then returned my gaze to Dylan, whose dress was working overtime to keep her contained. It was possible Lambert had sent her the Champagne.

I waited for André to sit, then slid into the banquette after him.

The waiter filled our glasses, then settled the bottle into the ice bucket more gently than new mothers settled their babies into bassinets.

"*Merci*," I told him.

"What about my martini?" asked Dylan. "Where's my martini?"

The waiter looked down at his nose at her. "*Un moment, mademoiselle.*"

"What did he say?"

"It will be here in a minute," André translated.

"I don't see why he has to be so rude and superior." Dylan's lower lip extended in a becoming pout. "Not everyone likes Champagne."

André patted her hand. "French waiters are rude to foreigners. It's part of their job description."

"Don't leave him a tip."

It wasn't worth the effort to explain his tip was included in the bill. Instead, I lifted the champagne flute, admired the bubbles, then tilted the glass toward the man who'd sent the wine. I even added a hint of a smile.

Ghislain Lambert said something to the people at his table, then rose, walking toward us with a supremely confident expression on his handsome face.

André leaned toward me and whispered in my ear. "That's the one?"

"Shhhh."

"You have excellent taste."

"Just wait till we get to Hermés." I swallowed a laugh at the expression on André's face, then I looked up at the man standing next to our table. "*Merci. Vous êtes trés gentil.*"

"Vous parlez Français?"

"Un peu." Actually, I spoke more than a little French. Chariss had dated a French director for a few years and I'd spent vacations in Paris, at his chateau in Biarritz, or at Hotel du Cap in Antibes. "May I thank you in English?"

"A woman as beautiful as you may say thank you in any language she wishes." Only a Frenchman could say something like that without sounding ridiculous.

"Please—" I waved at the banquette next to me "—join us."

He sat.

A waiter magically appeared with an extra Champagne glass and filled it with Krug.

"Where's my martini?" demanded Dylan.

The waiter sneered. *"Un moment."*

"He's sooo rude," said Dylan to his retreating back. She thrust her hand across the table and her substantial breasts nearly spilled out of her dress. "I'm Dylan Roberts."

"Ghislain Lambert." He took her fingers in his, shook once, then quickly released them.

"I'm Poppy Fields—" just in case he hadn't looked at a television or the internet in the past few weeks "—and this is my friend, André DuChamp."

"I've heard of you," said André. "We have a mutual client."

"Oh?" Ghislain raised his brows.

"Guy Lefebvre," said André.

"Ah. *Bien sûr.* I recognize your name. You represent his social media efforts." French disdain—Ghislain somehow managed to sound as if he was looking down his nose.

"You don't approve?" André could do disdain too. And there was no way some louche Frenchman would get away with insulting him.

"Like all good French fans, I want him to concentrate on fùtbol." He lifted his glass. "Shall we toast to—"

"Wait!" Dylan's shrill directive had dancers on the far side of the floor gaping at us. "I don't have a drink."

Ghislain caught the waiter's eye, nodded toward Dylan, and seconds later a martini appeared in front of her.

"You must come here often," I observed.

He shrugged, a Gallic shrug that said he regularly dropped tens of thousands of euros on an evening out. Ghislain lifted his glass and looked into my eyes. "To new friends."

We touched the rims of our glasses, then Ghislain turned to André and Dylan and touched the rims of their glasses.

The wine was divine. Thousand-dollar bottles of wine should be divine.

I sighed.

So did André. "That's amazing. Thank you."

"My martini is good, too."

Under the table, I tapped André's shin with the tip of my shoe, then jerked my head toward the dance floor.

"Dylan, would you like to dance?" André asked.

"Later." She slurped her martini and scanned the club, presumably looking for famous people with whom she could take selfies.

André shrugged. She'd said no, there was nothing he could do.

I leaned closer to him. "I'll forget about the scarves."

André's eyes widened. He sat straighter. He even rested his hand over Dylan's. "C'mon. Please? I love this song."

"Fine." She made dancing with one of the best-looking men in the club sound like an imposition.

André rose from his chair and held out his hand.

Dylan slurped again before she stood, smoothed her tiny dress over her tiny hips, and put her hand in his.

They walked into the crowd, where they were swallowed by lights and sound.

"Forget about the scarves?" asked Ghislain.

"A long story." Or not. André's dance with Dylan had cost me two beautiful squares of silk twill. "And a boring one. Tell me about yourself."

"I'm just a banker."

"A banker? You don't look like any bankers I know."

A satisfied smirk ghosted across Ghislain's lips.

"Most bankers don't send bottles of Krug Clos du Mesnil."

"Perhaps I'd like to have you as a client."

I brought the edge of the Champagne flute to my lips and stared into his eyes. "Perhaps we should talk about that."

"I'm having a party tomorrow night at my apartment in the Marais. Will you come?"

"Tomorrow night? I don't know…"

"Please, come."

"May I bring André?"

"You and DuChamp are—"

"Just friends."

"Then he is a fool."

I looked down at the table, unaccountably flustered. Frenchmen were so direct.

Ghislain lifted his glass from the table and I shifted my gaze back to him. He was watching the people on the dance floor. "By all means, bring DuChamp. Guy may be there." Now he looked into my eyes. "Give me your number and I'll text you the address."

"I don't give out my number." I mustered an apologetic smile. "You wouldn't believe how much reporters will pay for it." I had no idea how much they'd pay. I just didn't want to appear too eager. "If you want me to come tomorrow night, leave a message at the Ritz. I'll try to stop by."

Something like annoyance flashed across Ghislain's face. I was, after all, drinking the thousand-dollar-a-bottle Champagne he'd sent, the least I could do was agree to show up at his party.

"It's my mother. She keeps making plans for me."

"Your mother?"

Not for one minute did I believe he didn't know Chariss Carlton was my mother. Everyone in the world knew that. My mother was one of the biggest stars in Hollywood and I looked just like her. Seriously. It was spooky. But, for the sake of whatever information John Brown wanted me to find, I played along. "Chariss Carlton."

"Of course. I knew you looked familiar." He tilted his head to the side. "You're the woman who brought down a drug lord."

"I didn't bring down a drug lord. That was another cartel and a handful of government agents. I was just there for the shooting."

"But you survived."

"I kept my head down. And I ran."

"Someday you will have to tell me the story of how you escaped."

"Someday." When hell froze over.

He pulled the bottle of Krug from the ice bucket and refilled our glasses.

"Tell me, why are you in Paris?"

"Chariss is filming a movie. I'm spending a few days with her." I managed a giggle. "Of course, she works all day and is too tired to go out at night, so really we're just sharing a suite at the Ritz."

"Perhaps you'll bring her with you tomorrow night."

That wasn't going to happen, but I nodded. "Sometimes she insists I join her and her director for dinner." A total lie. When Chariss returned to the Ritz after work, she ordered a massage, a good Vouvray, and a piece of grilled chicken with rabbit food on the side. "I'll see if she feels like a party when she gets back from the shoot."

The song melted into another one.

"Your friends are returning." Ghislain stood. "I'll leave you to enjoy your evening."

"Thank you for the wine."

"You're welcome." He bent and kissed the air near my left cheek, then my right. "I'll see you tomorrow night."

Mr. Brown would be pleased. Things were going according to plan. But I shivered. Ghislain Lambert's parting words felt more like a threat than a promise.

TWO

Click-click-click. My dog's nails on the damp sidewalk melded with the sounds of passing cars, the drips of stray raindrops, and the muted hum of Paris at midnight.

I'd returned to my suite at the Ritz and found Consuela, the dog who'd adopted me in Mexico, in the mood for a late-night walk. Or maybe I was in the mood for a walk and Consuela was my excuse to take one.

We strolled past *Au Vieux Paris.* "Remind me to stop by here tomorrow." I'd noticed earrings the other day and their vintage sparkle had stayed with me—a sure sign they were meant to be mine.

"*Yip.*" Consuela liked shiny things. A lot. She was wearing a new collar set with faux amethysts that complemented her tawny fur, and if the jaunty way she lifted her paws was any indication, she liked her new bling immensely.

The sidewalk was quiet, few people were out, and the shops were shuttered.

"How 'bout we go to Café de la Paix?"

"*Yip, yip.*" For a Mexican dog, Consuela was fast developing a taste for tiny bites of French pastry.

We took a left on Avenue de L'Opéra, crossed Boulevard

des Capucines, and found a table outside under the café's green awning.

A waiter, looking spiffy in his black vest and apron, crisp white shirt, and gold tie, offered me a menu.

I waved it off. "*Non, merci. Je voudrais un chocolat chaud et* —" I looked down at the dog curled at my feet "—*un croissant.*"

"*Oui, mademoiselle.*"

I took out my cell and looked up Dylan's Instagram account. No surprise, she'd posted pictures of the two of us sitting on the banquette at Triomphe with the caption #*fun-withfriends*. Actually, the hashtag was a surprise. I hardly knew Dylan.

"*Yip.*" Consuela took a dim view of the time I spent on social media—it was time better spent paying attention to her.

I picked her up and she curled onto my lap with a contented sigh.

I slipped my cell into the pocket of my raincoat and looked around.

On the sidewalk, a man wearing sunglasses was staring at me.

I quickly shifted my gaze.

Also on the sidewalk, a model, dressed in black, impossibly thin and tall, with prominent cheekbones, sunken cheeks, and a hungry look in her eyes, walked by on the arm of a shorter man.

In the street, an ancient Peugeot stalled. The driver got out and opened the hood, prompting the cars behind him to honk.

The couple at the table next to mine argued in a language I couldn't identify. From their tones I surmised she was angry and he was making excuses. Some arguments were universal.

Aside from the man on the sidewalk (I peeked—he'd disappeared), Paris was ignoring me. I leaned back in my chair and enjoyed anonymity.

The waiter appeared with my hot chocolate and Consuela's croissant. "*Désirez-vous autre chose?*"

"*Non, merci.*"

I broke off a tiny piece of pastry and held out my fingers. Consuela sat up in my lap and, with unexpected delicacy, devoured the morsel.

She sighed and her eyes went all half-lidded and sultry as if French pastry was the ultimate pleasure.

Maybe Consuela was on to something. French pastry was a lot less complicated than other sultry pleasures. I took a tiny bite of croissant as well.

We sat and watched Paris for another twenty minutes— twenty minutes while I ignored the repeated buzzes in my pocket, refused to think about the last man who'd made my eyes go half-lidded and sultry, and considered Ghislain Lambert.

I'd googled him, so I'd expected handsome. I hadn't expected charming.

I bet he made plenty of women sigh like Consuela did when I slipped her another bite of croissant.

"Are you ready for bed?" Given the direction my thoughts had taken, it was a loaded question.

"*Yip.*"

I paid the bill and returned Consuela to the pavement.

She took a moment to stretch and yawn. She even offered up one last lingering look at the remaining croissant.

"It's bad for our waistlines," I told her.

She didn't answer. She merely trotted toward the exit, sure that I would follow. I might hold the leash, but she made the decisions.

Consuela paused outside the café, looked in all directions, then set off toward the Ritz via Boulevard des Capucines.

We passed Cartier and I ignored the siren call of its windows. I had to—Consuela was pulling on her leash as if she were in a hurry. She practically ran around the corner that led to Rue des Capucines.

And she wasn't done. Consuela tugged on her leash and looked over her shoulder toward the busier boulevard we'd left behind us. "*Yip, yip.*"

"Okay, okay." Obviously, my dog was ready for bed. That or she'd taken my waistline comment seriously and was burning off the extra calories. I trotted after her.

The narrow street was lined with parked cars. The quiet of an upscale neighborhood after midnight was velvety.

Consuela tugged.

I tugged back. How often did one get a whole street to oneself in Paris?

She stopped. Planting her little paws so suddenly I tripped over her.

My arms windmilled and I fell to the pavement.

"*Grrrr.*"

"It's your fault. You can't just stop like that." I rested on my knees and ignored the sting in my palms where my hands had skidded across the concrete. "Are you all right? Did I hurt you?"

"*Grrrr.*"

Twffft.

The store window next to me exploded.

I huddled over Consuela as bits of glass rained down upon us.

What had happened?

I looked up—looked out—into the street, where a black sedan I hadn't heard coming idled. "What the—"

Twffft.

The stone wall behind me sent sharp little shards my way.

Someone was shooting at me.

I sank back to the pavement with my heart beating triple-time in my throat.

I was on a deserted street. I had no weapon.

Traffic passed just fifteen feet ahead of me. But those fifteen feet might as well have been fifteen hundred. If the shooter stepped out of the car—when the shooter stepped out of his car—

I was dead.

Still, I had to try.

I pulled myself forward on my elbows and knees, dragging my body through the sea of broken glass. Next to me, Consuela picked her way through the debris.

I heard it—the sound of a car door opening.

My heart stopped for an instant. This was it. I rose to my knees, primed to run like hell as soon as I had a sense of where the shooter was.

The sweep of headlights flooded the street. Another car had come. And like the drivers behind the man in the ancient Peugeot, this driver didn't want to wait.

HOOONNK!

That honk was the most beautiful sound in the world. Well, next to the sounds of retreating footsteps and a car door slamming.

I didn't move. Didn't breathe. Not until the black sedan raced down the street and took a left. When its taillights disappeared, I jumped to my feet with Consuela in my arms and ran to the Ritz.

I burst through the doors but didn't feel safe until my heels sank into the red carpet covering the entrance stairs. I stumbled up the steps' broad length and stopped when I reached the lobby. I had to stop. My legs shook too hard to carry me forward.

The night manager, his face a mask of concern, hurried out from behind the discreet front desk. "Mademoiselle Fields?"

I didn't answer. I couldn't. I simply shook my head and looked down at my bloody knees.

With the gentlest of pressures on my elbow, the manager led me to a fauteuil, where I collapsed.

"Are you all right, Mademoiselle Fields?"

I stared up at him. He had a nice face—a face now wrinkled with concern.

"May I get you something?" he asked.

"Someone shot at me."

He raised a brow and his mouth opened as if he meant to respond but didn't know what to say.

"There's a window shot out on Rue des Capucines. The shooter was aiming at me."

He jerked his chin at a young woman hovering behind his shoulder. She dashed across the lobby and picked up a receiver. "The police will be here soon," said the manager. "And you are safe here. Would you like us to call your suite?"

And wake Chariss? When I was hardly bleeding?

"No."

Relief softened his features. Chariss was already displeased with the hotel. Some Russian oligarch was booked into her favorite suite and had refused to move. Instead of staying in the Imperial Suite, she had to make do with a suite inspired by Coco Chanel's former apartment. She wasn't happy about it.

The young woman returned and whispered in his ear.

"The police will be here any minute, Mademoiselle Fields."

I ran my shaking fingers through the softness of Consuela's fur and held her close. Someone had shot at me. Someone wanted me dead.

"I'm okay," I murmured. To my dog. To myself. I needed the reminder.

"Perhaps you'd care to wait in the Salon Proust. There will be fewer people walking by." The manager didn't add there'd be fewer chances for people to take pictures of me talking to a gendarme. Already the people who did pass through the lobby slowed to look at me. I couldn't blame them—a woman with torn clothes and bloodied palms was something of an anomaly at the Ritz.

My chin bobbed up and down and I rose from the fauteuil. "May I have a glass of water, please?" The rush of adrenaline had left my mouth dry.

"*Bien sur.*"

The manager led me to the intimate wood-paneled salon and saw me seated in one of the two gold brocade chairs flanking the fireplace. He flinched when Consuela jumped onto the other chair but held his tongue. Instead of telling me to remove my dog from the furniture, he rushed off to find me a Perrier.

I leaned my head against the back of the chair, closed my eyes, and concentrated on my breathing. My ability to fill my lungs came in fits and starts.

"Are you okay?"

I knew that voice. Too well. My eyes flew open.

Jake Smith, former boyfriend and fellow operative, stood in the doorway to the salon. Worry creased his face and his usual sunny aura had turned cloudy.

My head was too heavy to lift, so I left it where it was, pressing against the back of the chair. "What are you doing here?"

"You didn't answer my question."

I closed my eyes. "I'm fine."

"You don't look fine."

"Thanks."

"You have glass in your hair."

I touched my hair.

"And your pants are ripped."

He was right. The knees of my pants were shredded from my scramble across the glass-covered pavement.

"And you have that look."

"What look?" I snapped.

"Like you might be in shock."

"I'm not in shock." I sat up straight, opened my eyes, and scowled at him. "What are you doing here?"

"I saw it happen."

I took a few seconds to process that. "You were the honker?"

"The what?"

"You honked."

He nodded. "I did."

I should be grateful (definitely I should be grateful) but owing my uneven breaths to Jake wasn't a debt I welcomed. "And you came here to check on me rather than follow the shooter?"

His lips tightened.

"What?"

He shrugged. "I lost him."

"You lost him? Aren't you a highly trained operative?" As opposed to me, an untrained operative.

"Whoever he was, he was good."

"Any idea who it was?" Was it even a he? Women could shoot as well as men. "Did you get a plate number?" Another thought flashed across my brain. A thought that narrowed my eyes and tightened my hands into fists. "Were you following me?"

Jake flushed and shifted his gaze to Consuela.

He'd totally been following me.

"Why?" I demanded. "Why were you following me?"

"You're not cut out for this work. I was worried something would happen to you. And it did. If I hadn't been there, you'd be dead."

No way was I admitting he was right. Rather than look at him, I turned my gaze toward the gilt table in the center of the room. In the late afternoons, the hotel set the table for tea. "Go away."

"What?"

"You heard me."

"Why?"

Because he thought I couldn't take care of myself. Because he'd lied to me when we were dating, faked his own death, and let me grieve. Because he might swoop in to save me in a crisis, but otherwise he was completely unreliable. "Because."

"Poppy—"

I kept my gaze fixed on the table but held up a hand. "I don't want to hear it."

Grrrr. Neither did Consuela.

"Fine. I'll go, for now. But we need to figure out who wants you dead."

Who was he kidding? He knew the answer to that question. We both did. I glanced at him again, ignored the tiny flip of my heart, and gave him my best please-just-go-shrivel-up-and-die look. "There's only one person who might want me dead."

Jake opened his mouth as if he meant to respond, but voices (officious voices) carried toward us. Rather than saying something else to annoy me, Jake melted into the hallway.

A few seconds later, when the manager and a policeman with an Inspector Clousseau mustache entered the salon, Consuela and I were alone.

Grrrr. Consuela squinted at the police officer and bared her teeth. She didn't like men with mustaches.

The manager put a silver tray with an ice-filled glass and a bottle of Perrier on the side table next to my chair, then poured the water into the glass and handed it to me.

I drank. Deeply.

Meanwhile, the police officer extended his hand toward Consuela, foolishly ignoring her deepening growls and sharp teeth. "Does your dog bite?"

"Yes."

He snatched his hand away.

Just in time, too. Consuela looked as if she was about to do her best impression of a Tasmanian Devil.

It was not an auspicious start.

"Mlle. Fields, I am Inspector Forget." He presented me with a business card, then pulled a small pad of paper and pencil from his jacket pocket. "I understand someone shot at you?"

"Yes."

"On Rue des Capucines?"

"Yes."

Inspector Forget eyed the chair where Consuela perched, decided moving her might be dangerous to his health, and pulled a chair from a nearby table. He sat with a small grunt. "At what time did the incident occur?"

"Just before I ran into the lobby." I looked at the manager. "I'm not sure of the time."

"A few minutes before one," the manager supplied.

Inspector Forget made a note on his pad, then smoothed his mustache.

Grrrr.

"Consuela," I scolded. "Behave."

The inspector inched his chair farther away from my dog. "Can you think of anyone who might want to hurt you?"

I stared at the French detective, realized my mouth was hanging open, and snapped my lips shut.

"I take from your expression you do know someone. An ex-boyfriend?"

"No."

"Then who?"

Was he serious? "The current head of the Sinaloa drug cartel is not one of my fans."

He nodded and wrote. "Is that Sinaloa with an A or an O?"

"What?"

"How do you spell Sinaloa?"

"S-I-N-A-L-O-A."

He checked the spelling, erased a letter, and wrote a new one. "And why is that?"

"The former head of the cartel was killed after abducting me."

His brows, nearly as bushy as his mustache, rose. "You killed him?"

"Of course not."

"Then why?"

"It's a long story. You're going to have to take my word for it or—" I stifled my annoyance "—you can google me." Of course, the man was taking notes on paper—

maybe he was one of those people who hated technology.

"Who is this man who might want you dead?"

"Javier Diaz," I replied.

He nodded as if now we were getting somewhere. "I will find out if he has entered the country."

"He wouldn't do this himself." There was no way Javier would leave the relative safety of Mexico just to kill me. "If Javier wants me dead, there's a contract."

"A contract?"

"Yes."

Inspector Forget regarded me more closely. "You are involved in the drug trade?"

"No. I already told you, I was abducted by a drug lord."

The inspector pursed his lips and tapped his pencil against his pad.

"You can read about it online." I pulled my phone out of my pocket, opened a browser, and entered my name. I'd show him. Letting him read about what happened in Mexico was a million times easier than explaining it.

"You are sure there's no one else who wants you dead?"

I looked up from my cell. "I can't think of anyone." That Javier was willing to spend the money to have me killed came as a shock. Why bother? I glanced down at my phone and my heart stuttered. "Crap."

"What?"

Unable to speak, I handed him my cell.

Poppy Fields Escapes Paris Attacker. I was the lead story on TMZ.

How had they found out so fast?

I glared at the manager, who was looking over Inspector Forget's shoulder at the headline and wringing his hands.

A picture of me taken in the lobby only minutes ago came next.

"Someone—" Words failed me.

"Mademoiselle Fields, I am so sorry."

Blaming the manager would be easy and I desperately wanted someone to rage against, but neither the headline nor the picture were his fault. Anyone could have taken that picture. Anyone could have overheard me tell him about the gunshot—we hadn't whispered.

"Where is she?" A woman's voice carried down the hall.

Someone had awakened the dragon.

THREE

My mother, Chariss Carlton, swanned into the Proust Salon looking nothing like a dragon. She looked like an advertisement for luxury sleepwear. From the tips of her marabou puffed slippers to the top of her artistically tousled head, she was perfect. She leveled a deceptively wide-eyed gaze in my direction. "What happened? What's going on?"

"Someone shot at me."

Chariss sank gracefully into the nearest chair and covered her mouth with the tips of her fingers as if I'd given her shock.

The cynical part of me—the part of me that had spent years watching my mother effortlessly suck up all the oxygen in every room she ever entered—saw through her act. The freshly minted give-Chariss-a-chance part of me saw the hint of real concern in her eyes.

She perched on the edge of her chair, its cinnabar velvet setting off the soft pink of her peignoir. "Are you all right?"

"Fine. I scraped my knees." I glanced at my hands. "And my palms."

Across from me, Inspector Forget was doing an impression of a goldfish deprived of water. It was as if he'd never seen a woman who combined Brigitte Bardot's sex appeal, actress Cleménce Poésy's waif-like innocence, and style icon Charlotte Gainsbourg's offhand chic (it's not every woman whose mother has a Hermès bag named after her).

Maybe he hadn't. Chariss really was one of a kind. She stared at me—an accusing look that managed a you've-broken-my-heart quality—then looked down at her lap. "I got a call from California." She raised her eyes and her face was a mask of confusion. "Why didn't you wake me?" She was laying on the concerned-mother act a bit thick.

Then again, I was her toughest critic. "I didn't want to bother you." Truth was, Chariss was the last person I'd go to with a problem.

She shook her head as if I'd disappointed her—somehow hurt her by not calling her in a panic. "When did this happen?"

The manager glanced at his watch. "Less than an hour ago."

She pursed her lips, crossed her arms under her breasts, and shivered. Was she upset I hadn't come to her right away or that I'd nearly died?

"Casper called." Casper, otherwise known (to me) as the most annoying man on the planet, was Chariss's manager. The man never failed to inform her when I trended. Especially when I'd just as soon she not be informed. "I can't believe I had to hear about this from an employee." I had the answer to my question—she was annoyed because she'd heard about my little adventure from someone else.

"Someone took a photo of me in the lobby." I jerked my chin toward the hotel's entrance. "The pics are on TMZ already."

"I've asked Casper to arrange a bodyguard for you."

I stared at her, momentarily struck dumb.

Inspector Forget nodded as if Chariss were a genius.

I found my voice. "You didn't need to do that."

"Of course I did." Her voice had a sharp edge. Maybe she did care about someone shooting at me. At least a little.

But having a bodyguard provided by Chariss and Casper might make my job difficult. I opened my mouth, a second objection on my lips—

"I can't worry about you getting killed and shoot a movie. That's simply too much stress for me to handle."

There was the Chariss I knew. "Maybe they weren't trying to kill me. Maybe the shooting was random." I wasn't near the actress my mother was. I convinced no one.

Chariss didn't even bother dignifying my suggestion with a response. She merely shook her head and stood. "I insist that you have some protection. Now, I have an early call." She yawned in case I'd missed the unspoken message —she needed her beauty sleep and I'd disturbed her slumber.

Casper was the one who'd disturbed her slumber. I'd just been shot at.

Chariss stood. "If you gentlemen will excuse me…"

Of course they would.

She floated over to my chair and dropped a delicate kiss on the top of my head—a gesture totally for the benefit of the inspector and the manager. Chariss Carlton, doting mother. "Promise me you won't leave the hotel again tonight."

I looked down at my skinned knees. "I promise." Poppy Fields, obedient daughter.

We were both full of it.

Chariss disappeared in a swirl of satin. Only the lingering smell of her Fleurissimo remained.

The men watched her go. Then they watched the last place they'd seen her as if staring would make her come back.

I cleared my throat. Twice. "Do you have any more questions for me, Inspector Forget?"

He was still slack-jawed, wide-eyed, and sniffing the Chariss-scented air.

I hauled myself out of the chair. "If there's nothing further, I'd like to clean up."

The man merely nodded.

"Consuela, come."

Consuela hopped off her chair and trotted over to me.

"You'll let me know if you discover who shot at me?"

He didn't reply. He just sat there. Struck dumb.

I looked at the manager.

He was accustomed to dealing with Chariss and was less fazed be her marabou and satin and hypnotic charisma. "Goodnight, Mademoiselle Fields."

I gathered my dog into my arms and limped up the stairs to the Coco Chanel suite, where the door to Chariss's bedroom was firmly shut.

Just as well.

Consuela and I lingered at the window, looking down into Place Vendôme.

She twisted in my arms and licked my chin.

I kissed the top of her head (a sincere kiss—nothing delicate about it) and felt the phone in my pocket vibrate.

Consuela squirmed out of my arms and trotted into my bedroom.

I followed her.

She hopped up onto to her bed, circled three times, and curled into a small fluffy ball.

I closed the door, pulled the phone out of my pocket, and looked at the screen. I'd been expecting this call. "Hello."

"Someone tried to kill you." John Brown sounded only mildly interested.

"Yes."

"Who?"

I chose not to understand his question. "I didn't see the shooter."

On the other end of the line, he was shaking his head—I was sure of it. But, rather than remind me of all the reasons that Javier Diaz might want me dead, he said, "Jake couldn't catch the gunman."

"So he told me."

"Jake would have caught a *sicario*."

I didn't argue. Mainly because his point was so good. While Mexican hitmen were undeniably brutal and deadly, I couldn't imagine one who knew Paris streets well enough to escape Jake.

"That could mean only two things," he continued.

"Two?"

"Either Javier Diaz paid for a hit on you, or someone else wants you dead."

My bedroom was suddenly too cold. I sank onto the upholstered bench at the end of the bed and pulled a cashmere throw around my shoulders. "My mother's manager is arranging for a bodyguard."

John Brown laughed. At least that's what I thought the donkey-in-distress sound coming through the phone was.

"What's so funny?"

"Anyone your mother's people send will be ready to protect you from overzealous fans. This is a different kind of threat." He was right. Hollywood bodyguards were prepared for crazed stalkers, not hitmen.

"I don't think that's funny at all." So not-funny that the blood coursing through my veins had ice chips in it.

"I'll have someone there in the morning."

"Thank you."

"Spin this as a crazed stalker."

"Spin this?"

"We don't want anyone wondering why someone might want to kill you."

We didn't? Why not? "Spin this?"

"At some point in the next day, someone will shove a microphone in your face. Spin it."

I didn't care how the shooting was spun as long as the gunman was caught. "Fine."

"You met Ghislain Lambert tonight." Mr. Brown sounded pleased.

"That's what you sent me to do."

"Others have tried."

"He sent Champagne."

"Good."

"Expensive Champagne." I wasn't telling him anything he probably didn't already know.

"Better."

"He invited me to a party tomorrow night." I looked at the clock and corrected myself. "Tonight."

"Best."

"I told him I'd think about it."

"You what?" Mr. Brown's voice boomed through the phone, loud enough for Consuela to raise her little face from her paws and growl softly.

"I told him I'd think about it." I spoke slowly and pictured Mr. Brown making Inspector Forget's gasping-goldfish face.

"Why?"

"Because if it's easy to catch my attention, he'll lose interest."

A moment of silence followed. "You are going to the party?"

That had been my plan, but now—I thought before I answered. Someone had tried to kill me. They'd shot at me, and if Jake hadn't come along, I'd probably be dead. I held out my free hand and watched it tremble.

He sighed. "No one would blame you if you decide to go back to California."

He was offering me an out. But he was wrong about the blame thing.

If I tucked tail and ran back home, I'd blame me.

John Brown and his shadowy agency had offered me a

chance to make a difference—a chance I'd desperately wanted. Until, I'd run afoul of a Mexican drug lord, I'd floated through my life. After I'd helped take down said drug lord, I knew my life could have meaning. If I ran away the first time things got dangerous, I'd never be able to live with myself. "I'm definitely going to that party. I'll take André and my new bodyguard." I watched my hand tremble for a few more seconds, then tightened my fingers into a fist. "Make sure he's handsome."

"What?"

"The bodyguard. Make sure he's handsome."

"Why?"

"Because I want Lambert to wonder if I'm sleeping with him."

"Very well. I'll send you Stone." With that cryptic comment he hung up.

KNOCK, knock.

I rolled over, grabbed for my phone, and looked at the time.

"Ugh."

Knock, knock.

I rolled out of bed, jammed my arms into one of the Ritz's fluffy robes, and staggered out of my bedroom and to the suite's door.

Consuela followed me, yawning all the way.

Knock, knock.

"Coming." I yanked open the door.

"Miss Fields—" the man in the hallway extended his right hand "—I'm Mark Stone."

Mark Stone looked more like Chris Hemsworth than Chris Hemsworth. John Brown hadn't sent me a bodyguard; he'd sent me Thor.

Dumbstruck, I extended my fingers.

His hand swallowed mine.

"Nice to meet you," I murmured. "Come in."

He followed me into the suite Chariss and I shared. "Nice digs."

Coco Chanel had lived in the hotel. For thirty years. When the Ritz remodeled, they'd quietly moved the elegant furnishings which retained her spirit to another floor. The new Coco Chanel suite was decorated in shades of ecru and white accented with black lacquer screens and gilded mirrors. It was costing the production company a small fortune (more than twenty thousand dollars a night) to keep Chariss sleeping in Coco-inspired quarters.

Chariss much preferred the over-the-top luxury of the Imperial Suite, but I didn't complain.

"Did I wake you?" he asked.

"I had a rough night." I'd spent long hours staring at the ceiling wondering if Javier Diaz really wanted me dead. And if he didn't, who did? "I need some breakfast. Would you like anything?"

"Coffee. Please."

I picked up the phone. *"Bonjour, je voudrais une corbeille du boulanger, un café latte et un—un moment, s'il vous plait."* I turned to Thor. "Regular coffee? Espresso? Cappuccino?"

"Just coffee."

I spoke into the phone. *"—et un café American. Merci."*

I put the receiver back in its cradle.

"Who's the pooch?"

"This is Consuela."

Thor held out his hand and Consuela sniffed.

She didn't growl or snap. She merely turned up her nose.

"She likes you."

He raised a single brow. "Could have fooled me."

"Trust me. That's as warm as Consuela ever gets with

strangers." I settled onto the velvet couch. "I've never had a bodyguard. How does this work?"

"Where you go, I go."

"And that's it?"

"I don't let anyone hurt you."

"I don't have to change my schedule?"

"I'd prefer it if you avoided large crowds."

"So no trips to the Louvre?"

He looked pained.

"Do you have something against the Mona Lisa?"

"She draws a crowd."

"I think we can avoid museums."

He nodded his thanks. "What's on your schedule today?"

"Let me grab my phone." I padded into my bedroom, grabbed my cell off the bedside table, and opened the calendar. "This morning, I need to go to Antoine Gabriel's atelier. In fact—" I stood, tightening the belt of my robe "—I should probably get dressed while we're waiting on breakfast."

I left him with Consuela and jumped in the shower.

Twenty minutes later, dressed in boyfriend jeans, a cashmere sweater, and Tod's loafers I could run in, I paused at the door from my bedroom to the main salon. There were voices on the other side.

And Chariss's was one of them.

I cracked the door.

Thor was sipping coffee and looking out the window at Place Vendôme.

Chariss was staring at him over the rim of my café latte. "Where exactly did you come from?"

Would he say Asgard?

"Cleveland."

"How did you get here?" Chariss insisted.

If he said by chariot, I was going to kiss him.

"I work for an agency back in the states. Poppy called someone she knows at the DEA and they suggested me."

"Poppy called someone?" Chariss sounded surprised.

"She knew you were concerned."

"Someone *shot* at her."

I cleared my throat. "What are you doing here, Chariss?"

She considered my outfit with narrowed eyes. "We filmed at dawn. When the light changed, Franco took a break. I came back to check on you. But—" Chariss's gaze slid toward Thor and a smile touched her lips "—it seems as if you have things well in hand."

Chariss might have my latte, but the basket of pastries still waited for me on the table in front of the couch. I sat down and helped myself to a croissant. "When do you have to be back on set?"

Chariss put my cup down and glanced at her watch. "I've got about an hour. What are you doing today?"

"I'm due at Antoine Gabriel's atelier by noon. Tonight I'm going to a party."

"Do you think that's wise?"

"I'll take care of her, Ms. Carlton." Of course he would. He was a Norse god.

Chariss did that wide-eyed, fluttery-lash that usually brought men to their knees. "Call me Chariss."

Thor seemed unaffected. Interesting.

"Also, André is taking me to Hermès."

"Oh?" Chariss floated over to the couch, settled onto its cushions, and took the croissant from my hands. "Why?"

"He's buying me a bag."

"How nice of him." She pulled one of the points off my croissant and popped it in her mouth.

I eyed the bread basket. They'd only sent one croissant.

"So, a fitting and a trip to Hermès? Not the most exciting day for you, Mark."

"I prefer days that aren't exciting." If the bodyguard thing didn't work out, Thor could pursue a career in diplomacy. Or modeling.

"Then you're guarding the wrong woman." Chariss looked down her perfect nose at the remains of my croissant. "Poppy attracts trouble like carrion attracts vultures."

Carrion? Had she really just compared me to rotting flesh?

Thor, who was standing next to the window, made a noise in his throat that sounded suspiciously like a swallowed guffaw. "I can handle trouble, Ms. Carlton."

"I'm sure you can." Chariss leaned back. "And I asked you to call me Chariss."

"I can handle trouble, Chariss." He shifted his gaze to the Place, as if he were scouting for potential threats.

Unaccustomed to men who ignored her, Chariss brushed her fingers across her lips and leaned forward enough to reveal a hint of cleavage. "What do you do when you're not guarding people?"

With his gaze still on the Place, Thor replied, "My job keeps me busy."

"No hobbies?"

Now he turned and looked at her. "I like guns."

Chariss, whose current film project had her waving a Glock around in every other scene, curled her upper lip into a becoming sneer. "Guns? Really?" Movie guns were one thing, but real ones—they were a no-no. "What else?"

"I practice Krav Maga."

With an oh-so-delicate tilt of her chin, Chariss shifted her attention to me. "Isn't that what your father made you learn?"

"He didn't make me."

The line of her lips hardened—for a fleeting instant—then gave way to her most charming smile. "Mark, would you please bring me my coffee?"

My coffee.

Arguing would get me nowhere. I'd let her drink the whole thing, then tell her it wasn't made with skim milk.

Thor brought her the cup.

She settled back on the couch and sipped. "If you're not

busy, you could stop by the set this afternoon." Chariss was up to something.

"I thought you were worried about Th—Mark being bored."

She wrinkled her nose at me. "Some people find movie-making fascinating."

I wasn't one of them. And she knew it. Which meant…

"How old are you, Mark?" My non-sequitur question hung in the air.

Thor looked at me with a bemused expression on his Norse-god face. "Thirty-one. Why?"

"Just wondering."

He shrugged his enormous shoulders and returned to the window and his careful scan of the Place.

Thor might not understand why I'd asked his age, but Chariss (who had cougar tendencies) did. If she wanted to fool around with a younger man, she could find one who wasn't tasked with protecting me.

She gave me a look the movie-going public never saw. Her eyes were slits, her teeth were bared, and her cheeks were flushed. As far as I could tell, that look was her first genuine expression of the morning—and it said she'd like to kill me.

She'd have to get in line.

FOUR

Established ateliers—Dior, St. Laurent, and Courreges—clustered in the *Triangle d'Or*, or Golden Triangle, between Avenues Montaigne, George-V, and the Champs-Élysées. The grande-dame of ateliers, Chanel, held court on rue Cambon. The addresses were as chic as the clothes. And they were in the opposite direction.

My fitting was with a new designer, one whose atelier was near the considerably less chic Les Halles, a thousand-year-old market.

Thor, Consuela, and I climbed into a taxi and I gave the driver the address.

The taxi driver responded with drawn brows and a very Parisian grunt (apparently, he didn't appreciate dogs in his car).

"Where are we going?" Thor stared out the window, carefully scanning our surroundings. "Antoine Gabriel's atelier."

He turned his head toward me. "Atelier?"

"His studio."

"I thought we were going to a dress shop."

"We are."

"But you said studio." Thor twisted his shoulders and

neck and looked out the back window. "Aren't those for artists?"

"Antoine is an artist." I followed his gaze. "Are you looking for something in particular?"

"Just making sure no one is following us."

"Are they?"

His shoulders relaxed. "I don't see anybody. You have a special occasion?"

"No. Why?"

"New clothes."

"No occasion. It's just a couple of dresses."

"For no reason?" Was that judgment I heard in his voice?

"For no reason," I confirmed. "Except, I like Antoine and me being seen in his clothes will help him."

Thor looked doubtful. "Help him how?"

Warmth crept up my neck and into my cheeks. "There are people who pay attention to who I wear—" I looked out the window, unwilling to meet his gaze "—and where and I go and…"

"How do they know where you go?" Thor's voice was sharp, all judgment gone.

"Sometimes I post a picture. Sometimes I get tagged."

"Tagged?"

Apparently, John Brown's operatives didn't spend a lot of time on Instagram. "Tagged. On social media. And there's the paparazzi…"

"Did you post where you were last night? That you were going for a walk?"

"No. Of course not." I thought for a moment. "Dylan was posting pics of me as if I was still with her. Anyone following her on Instagram would have thought I was at a club. Whoever shot at me must have followed me from the hotel, spotted me at Café de la Paix, or seen me on the sidewalk."

"Dylan who?"

"Dylan Roberts. She was on…" I still couldn't recall the name of her show. "She's a reality star."

"A what?"

Did the man live under a rock? "A reality star. She's on a reality show."

"I don't watch much TV."

Apparently not.

"You and Dylan are friends?"

"I hardly know her."

"You go clubbing with people you hardly know?"

"I went with André DuChamp. He brought Dylan."

"Who's André DuChamp?"

"One of my best frie—"

A Citroën cut in front of us. Our driver slammed on the taxi's brakes, honked, and stuck his head out the window. "*Putain!*"

Thor reached inside his jacket.

Consuela, who sat between us, growled.

My breath caught and I clenched my hands into fists. Was it happening again? Was someone going to shoot at us?

The driver of the Citroën gave the little car some gas and it shot ahead of us.

Thor took his hand out of his jacket.

I breathed again.

The taxi driver glanced in the rearview mirror and said, "*Ce mec conduit comme un fou.*"

"*Oui.*" I nodded my agreement and relaxed my fingers.

"What did he say?" asked Thor.

"The other driver was crazy."

A few minutes later, the taxi delivered us to Antoine's atelier. I paid the fare, and we climbed out of the taxi.

Consuela stopped and sniffed the trunk of a horse chestnut tree.

Thor took my arm. "We should get inside."

"Fine." I tugged gently on Consuela's leash.

Thor pushed open the door to Antoine's storefront.

I breezed past him and found the front room empty. "Antoine?" I called. "*Es-tu ici?*"

Thor followed me inside and gaped as if he'd never been in a boutique before. Maybe he hadn't. Or maybe he'd never seen one like Antoine's. The floor was black concrete polished to an impossibly high shine. The walls were painted the palest shade of shell pink. A chandelier dripping thousands of crystals hung from an exposed structural beam. Velvet poofs two shades darker than the walls dotted the floor. Two gilt fauteuils upholstered in camouflage flanked the three-way mirror. Champagne (Pol Roger, not Krug) chilled on a bar cart.

On this, the prêt-à-porter side of his space, Antoine sold tulle skirts paired with vintage T-shirts, pencil-leg pants coupled with oversized trench coats, linen scarves in ice-cream hues, and jean jackets hand embroidered with wild, colorful designs.

"Antoine?" I called.

There was still no answer.

I tried again. "Gaston?" Gaston was Antoine's partner in business and in life.

He didn't answer either.

Consuela sniffed and growled deep in her throat.

Thor reached inside his jacket and jerked his head toward the door to the street. He wanted me to leave.

I nodded. Something was off, and chills were creeping and crawling up and down my neck. "Fine. Let's go."

My hand closed around the door handle.

"Wait!" Antoine exploded through the rose velvet curtain hiding the hallway to his work room and stumbled over his own feet. "I thought I heard you." His usually cultured voice was unnaturally high, his hair was mussed, and there was a crazed look in his eyes.

"Is everything all right?" I asked. "*Ça va?*"

"Everything is fine. Perfect now that you're here." Antoine pulled me into a hug and kissed the air next to my cheek. "You are—" his voice was barely a whisper. He switched cheeks "—in danger."

Again?

He moved in for the third kiss and I murmured, "What's happening?"

His answer was a tiny jerk of his head toward the curtain.

"Where's Gaston?"

Tears welled in his eyes.

My insides chilled as if they were being flash-frozen. "I know I have clothes to try on—" I spoke at regular volume in case we were being watched or listened to "—but I want to see those jackets. They're new since I was last here." They weren't. "They're gorgeous." They were. "I might be obsessed."

I grabbed Antoine's arm and led him toward the embroidered denim. "Tell me about this one." I held up a jacket with a dragon winding across its back and hid our faces from anyone watching from the work room. "Is he all right?"

"They have him tied up." Antoine covered his mouth with his hand and squinched his eyes closed. "They have a gun to his head."

"Why?"

"They want you." Antoine's voice was watery.

My heart stuttered to a momentary stoppage. "How many?"

"*Trois*. Three."

"Mark," I trilled. "Come here. I need your opinion."

Thor, who'd been standing by the door, alternating between frowning at Antoine and scowling at passersby on the pavement outside the store, walked over to the display of jean jackets.

"I want to try this one." I turned my back on the curtain and pulled the dragon embroidered jacket on over my sweater. "There are three bad guys in the back," I whispered. "They're holding Antoine's partner."

Thor didn't react. His expression remained the same. There was no sudden stiffness in his shoulders, no tightening near his eyes. He simply said, "You need to get out of here."

"No!" Antoine shouted. All the color bled out of his cheeks. He glanced over his shoulder at the curtain, then grabbed another jacket and thrust it into my hands. "This is the one for you. I'll help you." He moved behind me, yanking the dragon jean jacket I was wearing away from my shoulders. "They said if you walked out the front door, if I warned you, they'd kill him."

And he'd warned me anyway.

Why hadn't the men in back just shot me? Here in the store, I was an easy target.

I glanced at Thor. "We have to help Gaston."

He shook his head. "My job is to protect you."

As if I'd leave a friend in trouble. "You know—" I put a smile in my voice "—I think you're right, Antoine." I moved toward the three-way mirror. "This jacket is fabulous. If you pour me a glass of Champagne, the decision to buy it will be easier."

Both men looked at me as if I'd lost my mind, but Antoine poured wine into a flute and handed it to me.

"*Merci*." I walked toward the curtain, stopping only to tell Consuela, "Do *not* follow me."

"Poppy." There was a warning in Thor's voice.

Yip. There was a warning in Consuela's bark. She had no intention of minding me. I scooped her up and handed her to Antoine. "Keep her safe," I whispered. Then, louder, I added, "I'll only be a minute." I pulled back the curtain.

Thor reached for me.

I slipped through his grasp and into the hallway.

The empty hallway.

I hurried down its length toward Antoine's workroom.

Thor caught me, his hand like a shackle around my arm. "What the hell do you think you're doing?"

Were we being watched?

"I'm not done yet, dear." I smiled up at him and took a sip of Champagne. "This fitting won't take long."

He tugged me in the other direction.

I narrowed my eyes. "I know you're dying to get to the Louvre, but I simply must get those dresses fitted."

He bent down and whispered, "This is too dangerous."

"The only way you're getting me out of here is if you drag me," I whispered back.

"And I thought your mother was a pain in the ass."

"You did?" For a moment I forgot all about poor Gaston. Thor had seen through Chariss? Men never saw through Chariss.

"She drank your coffee. She ate your croissant. She hit on your bodyguard." He tugged on me again.

"You're a very nice man, but I'm not leaving."

He muttered something about me getting us both killed.

I shook off his grasp and took another step. "Gaston?" I called. "Antoine said you'd pin me. Where do you want me?"

"In here." Gaston's pitch was strangled and high.

I drained my Champagne and broke the flute against the wall.

Thor just rolled his eyes. What good was one broken bit of crystal against three killers? At least he held a Glock.

"Poppy?" Gaston called. "What happened?"

"I'm so sorry, Gaston. The glass slipped through my fingers. Do you have a broom?"

"It doesn't matter."

I closed my hand around the curtain and yanked.

There were three men—just as Antoine had said. One beefy, one scrawny, one scarred. The beefy one held a gun to Gaston's head. The other two pointed guns at me.

They hadn't counted on Thor.

Bang.

He shot the scarred man, the one nearest me.

The body thudded to the floor before I had time to blink.

The scrawny man swung the muzzle of his gun away from me and pointed it at Thor.

A long second passed and no one moved. I didn't breathe.

A trickle of sweat ran down the scrawny man's temple.

The beefy man with the gun pressed to Gaston's head watched with a mixture of horror and rage on his face.

The men were at an impasse.

I was not. I lunged forward. The sharp edges of the jagged Champagne flute met the beefy man's throat and entered his skin. Sickening.

He made a bloody, bubbly sound, dropped his gun, and clasped the glasses stem with both hands.

I scrabbled for his pistol, slipped in the scarred man's blood, and landed on my bruised knees. *Hell!* I stretched and grabbed for the gun.

Too late. When I flipped over, the scrawny man had a Glock pointed at my forehead.

Bang!

The gunshot reverberated off the concrete floors—reverberated through my spine and heart and lungs.

The scrawny man toppled to the floor.

Gaston's eyes rolled back in his head and his chin fell forward. He'd reached his limit of guns and death. He was out cold.

Thor stepped over the scrawny man's body and grabbed the bleeding beefy man. "Who sent you?"

"*Alluha Akbar.*" The man reached into the pocket of his jacket and pulled out a wicked knife.

"Watch out!" I lifted the pistol I'd recovered from the floor and pulled the trigger.

The light faded from the beefy man's eyes as crimson blossomed across his chest. Thor was left holding dead weight.

"Dammit!" Thor's cheeks flushed a deep red and the space above his nose furrowed until his brows touched.

I scooted away—from him and from the growing sea of blood. "He was going to stab you."

"He had information." Thor let the beefy man's body fall to the floor. "You ever seen any of these guys before?"

"No." I'd been expecting *sicarios.* The dead men looked Middle Eastern.

He rubbed the back of his hand across the bridge of his nose, then kicked a blameless poof. "Dammit, dammit, dammit!"

The poof tipped and rolled through a pool of blood.

I didn't move.

Thor scanned the dressing room, spotted a black nylon duffle, and ripped it open. "What the—"

"What?" My voice was barely there.

He held up a bag of zip ties and a roll of duct tape.

That made no sense. They wanted me dead. Why bother with the accoutrements of a kidnapping?

"What kind of gun is that?" Thor demanded.

I glanced down at the pistol still gripped in my hand and squinted at the engraving. "Ed Brown."

"May I see it?" His voice was tight, controlled.

I held the gun out to him.

He took it and his eyes narrowed. "This is a Special Forces Carry."

"I don't know what that means."

"It's expensive. It costs upwards of two thousand dollars."

I waited for him to tell me more.

His lips thinned till they disappeared. "These guys weren't well trained. And—" he used the gun's muzzle to point at the baggie of zip ties "—they weren't here to kill you. So how did they get their hands on a top-of-the-line gun?"

I wasn't worried about the label on the gun—my mind was still on the zip ties. "What's going on?"

"I don't know."

Gaston moaned.

I'd forgotten all about him. I stumbled to his chair. His hands were tied behind his back. "Gaston, are you all right?"

He groaned again and opened his red-rimmed eyes. "Antoine? Is he—"

"He's fine."

"Thank God." Gaston closed his eyes on the carnage.

I couldn't blame him for closing his eyes. Antoine's work-room looked like something from a nightmare—awash with blood and scented with death. I swallowed. "Tho—Mark, is there a knife in that bag?"

Thor opened the bag wider and dug out a wicked-looking dagger.

"Would you please cut Gaston loose?"

Thor cut the ties.

With his arms free, Gaston hugged himself. And shook. Like a leaf.

"What are we going to do about this?" I asked.

"This?"

How could Thor not understand *this?* There were three bodies at our feet. I was responsible for one of them. I waved my hand at all of them.

He rubbed his chin, considering. "I'll call Mr. Brown. He knows someone at the National Police."

"The National Police?"

"It's like the French FBI."

"Maybe you should call Mr. Brown now. Right away."

He stared at me for a long second, then nodded and took a few steps toward the hall.

"Mark—"

He stopped walking.

"How did they know I'd be here?"

He tilted his head. "What do you mean?"

"These guys were waiting for me. I've never posted about

coming here. I've never mentioned Antoine or his clothes. How did they know I was coming?"

Thor scowled at Gaston. "Did you or your partner—"

"We would never!" Gaston sounded outraged.

"Ever!" Antoine had ventured down the hallway. He held Consuela, squirming in his arms.

Yip!

Antoine put my dog down and hurried to Gaston's side. "Are you all right?" Ignoring the blood on the floor, he fell to his knees and wrapped his arms around his partner's waist.

Gaston lowered his forehead until it brushed the top of Antoine's head. "I'm all right, thanks to Poppy and her friend."

If it weren't for me, they wouldn't have been in danger.

Yip. Consuela sat at my feet, demanding my attention. I picked her up and she licked my chin.

"Did any of these men say what they wanted?" Thor looked very Thor-like with his shoulders thrown back and his feet planted just beyond the gore.

"They wanted Poppy," Gaston replied.

Guilt twisted inside me. The men had come for me, but they'd terrorized Gaston and Antoine.

Yip. Consuela had no patience for guilt.

"What exactly did they say?" Thor insisted.

Gaston shook his head. "They mainly spoke Arabic."

Antoine nodded. "The only time they spoke French was when they told me they'd kill Gaston if Poppy left."

"How did they know I'd be here?" I really wanted an answer to that question.

"Maybe they hacked your cell," said Antoine. "I read about that happening in *Le Figaro*. Do you keep a calendar on your phone?"

I did.

I pulled my phone out of my pocket and opened the calendar. There it was, the only entry for today: Antoine Gabriel's, with his address and a timeframe. My fingers tightened, and I drew my arms back, ready to throw the phone to the concrete floor and grind it to dust beneath my heel (or maybe Thor's heel—my Tod's weren't really made for destroying electronics).

"Wait!" Thor held up a hand, stopping me.

"Why?" I felt as if the cell in my palm had betrayed me.

"They can track me."

"Yeah, and we can set a trap."

FIVE

There were other places in the world where the weather balanced between mist and light rain, but to me, the phenomenon was quintessentially Parisian.

I looked out from under my umbrella and asked Thor, "Have you been to Hermès before?"

"No."

Thor didn't look like the kind of man who enjoyed shopping. In fact, he was eyeing the carved wooden storefront with a deep furrow in his forehead.

I pushed open the door. "This is the original store. When it was founded, Hermès made harnesses."

"Harnesses?"

"For horses. Then saddles. Then bags to carry the saddles. Then bags for women to carry."

Thor didn't look particularly interested.

We stepped inside the store, where leather goods were displayed like pieces of fine art.

Thor didn't look particularly impressed. Then again, his plan had been for me to spend the rest of the day at the Ritz. In the suite. With the door locked.

There was probably some sense to his plan—erring on the side of caution—but it felt like hiding.

And I didn't want to hide.

Besides, André was on the hook for a handbag.

"This won't take long," I promised.

"Yeah, right." It was as if he didn't believe me—as if women had promised him brief shopping trips before. "Just stay alert."

André, who stood at a counter with a half-dozen ties spread across its surface, noticed me and waved. Then he noticed Thor and his wave stuttered and stopped.

I swallowed a sigh and walked over to him.

"You look tired," André observed before turning to Thor. "I'm André DuChamp."

"Mark Stone."

"Are you the reason Poppy looks tired?"

"André!" I punched my friend in the arm. Hard. "Mark is my bodyguard."

André's brows waggled. "Your bodyguard?"

"My bodyguard. Chariss insisted."

"Sure she did." André's smirk became a leer.

"I'm serious. After last night, she said she'd be too worried to act if I didn't have a guard."

"What happened last night?"

"Haven't you looked at the internet?" It was his *job* to look at the internet.

André yawned, covering his mouth with the back of his hand. "I just got up."

"Someone shot at me last night."

"Poppy!" His hands circled my arms and he stared down at me. "What happened? Are you all right?"

"I'm fine."

"Who shot at you? Did they catch the guy?"

"No idea and no."

His gaze darted around the elegant store as if there might

be assassins hiding behind the mannequins. "Is it safe for you to be out? You should be back at the hotel."

Thor snorted. His thoughts exactly.

"We don't need to do this today." André actually took a step toward the door.

"Don't be silly. Nothing bad ever happens at Hermés."

Thor snorted again.

"What about that party you told me about? You can't go to that party."

Attending Ghislain Lambert's party was my job. Going to the party could be a major step in learning what he was up to. "Why not?"

"Uh, hello! Someone shot at you."

"They missed. I'm going." I had things to prove. To myself and to Mr. Brown.

André rubbed his chin, then looked down at the display of colorful silk. "I can't go with you."

The clerk who'd been waiting on André, one of those Parisian women who had chic running through her veins instead of blood, shifted the ties.

I'd been counting on him. "Why not?"

"It's complicated."

With André, things were always complicated. "What's his name?"

"It's not that."

"Then what?"

André shook his head, suddenly mute.

I smiled at the clerk. "I'd like to see a Toolbox Twenty-Six in bleu atoll, please."

"*Bien sûr.*"

She left us, and I focused on André. "If it's not a new man, what is it? Why can't you go with me?"

André's lips thinned and he glanced at Thor. "Could you give us a minute?"

Thor backed up. Choosing a spot near the door, he crossed

his arms and looked menacingly at anyone within fifteen feet of me.

"He looks like Chris Hemsworth," André whispered.

"I'm aware." I wasn't about to let André change the subject. "What do you mean you're not coming tonight?"

"I can't."

"Why not?"

"It's Dylan."

He was blowing me off for Dylan? "I can't wait to hear this."

Either André was obsessed with the ties displayed on the counter or he didn't want to look me in the eye. His gaze remained fixed. "I can't bring her. She'd be a disaster at a party like that, and I can't leave her alone all night. The woman doesn't know anyone in Paris and she's staying in an awful hotel and—"

"Why is she here? In Paris? With you?"

A flush colored André's cheeks and he stroked a salmon-hued tie with the tip of his finger. "I have a concept for a new reality series. It's about an American who travels the world looking for luxury experiences. The kicker is she's never been out of the country before, so everything is new and fresh and exciting. The Travel Channel is interested."

I stared at him. "So it's a show about a wide-eyed tourist?"

"Kinda." He nodded without shifting his gaze.

"One who makes mistakes? Asks for the bathroom instead of *la toilette*?"

"Exactly." He moved his fingertip to a pale pink tie.

"So viewers learn how not to do things by watching her screw up?"

His shoulders rose and fell. "I guess."

"Does Dylan understand she's the ugly American in this scenario?"

André stiffened. "Dylan isn't remotely ugly."

"You know what I mean." The French would think she

was gauche. The British would think she was brash. The Germans would think she was naïve. They'd all be right. "So where are you going tonight?"

"A private tour of the catacombs. Believe me—" he finally looked up at me "—I'd rather be with you."

I actually did believe him. Not only was André mildly claustrophobic, he was also afraid of cemeteries. There had to be a lot on the line for him to willingly enter the catacombs, the subterranean resting spot of millions of French bodies displaced by the living's need for space.

"You understand, don't you?"

The clerk reappeared with the handbag and put it on the counter in front of us.

It was my turn to run the tip of my finger across luxury goods. *"C'est parfait. Monsieur DuChamp va l'acheter pour moi."*

The clerk's face remained impassive as she waited for approval from André.

"Yeah." He sounded only mildly put upon. "And I'll take the ties."

"Which ones, monsieur?"

"All of them."

"You don't wear ties." My point was a good one.

"I know, but who can resist?" So very André. Generous to a fault, the man spent money as fast as he made it. What did he plan on doing with a thousand dollars' worth of ties he'd never wear?

The ties were none of my concern. "Back to this trip to the catacombs." There had to be a better reason for him to go than keeping Dylan company when she went underground. "What's up with that?"

"Just a sec." He handed the clerk a black American Express and watched her carefully drape the ties over her arm, collect my bag, and walk away. "I'd get to produce."

"You? Produce?"

"Shhh." He scowled at me and glanced at the other

customers to see if any of them had overhead. André's father had produced one of the biggest flops in Hollywood history. The fallout had left André scarred.

"Sorry," I whispered. "You're going to produce?"

"It's just a reality show." He stared at a saddle on the other side of the store. Stared hard. "But I have to try."

"I guess I understand." Sort of. My creative parent, Chariss, was not the one I tried to emulate. I felt no need to act. If I could choose to be like one of my parents, it would be my father. He was Special Forces before he met my mother. He gave it up for her. And she left him—left us—the minute a pilot she'd made got picked up. For thirteen years, it was me and my dad in Montana. I'd learned to ride and shoot and just be a kid. Then a man with a gray face and gray suit knocked on the door and told me Dad's plane had gone down. That's when Chariss had reentered my life. "If I were you, I wouldn't make the show about luxury. That's been done a thousand times. I'd make it about urban exploring."

"Huh?" André's expression said I'd sprouted a second head.

"Urban exploring. Have Dylan go scuba diving in the tunnels beneath Paris. I've heard there's a secret metro line under Moscow. There has to be something interesting underneath London. There are roof toppers in Shanghai."

"Roof toppers?"

"They climb skyscrapers." I shrugged. "Dylan could, too. You could team her up with explorers in different cities. That would be a lot more interesting than watching her eat *foie gras* surrounded by all the skulls stored in the catacombs."

André opened his mouth—no doubt ready with a smart remark about how stupid my idea was—but the impossibly chic clerk returned with two of Hermès's signature orange shopping bags.

She handed me the larger one.

"*Merci.*" I accepted the bag and turned to André. "Thank you."

He shrugged. "It's the least I could do. One of the photos of you and Dylan trended. By the time I went to bed last night, she'd picked up twenty thousand new followers."

"Think about the urban explorer thing."

"I will if you promise you'll be careful tonight."

"I'm always careful." My thoughts returned to the blood-soaked atelier. Thor hadn't thanked me for shooting Beefy. Then again, I hadn't thanked him for saving me from Scarred or Scrawny.

"You're never careful."

"Well, I will be tonight." I raised up on my tiptoes and kissed his cheek. "Promise."

Thor and I made it back to the hotel without anyone shooting at me. That counted as a win. Our taxi stopped and a throng of paparazzi surrounded the car.

Twenty-five men with cameras pushed against the windows.

"What do they want?"

"Me." It was the simple answer.

"Why?"

"Someone tried to kill me last night. The whole world is wondering if Javier Diaz wants me dead." I tilted my head and looked at the roof of the taxi. "If he succeeds, these pictures will be worth a fortune."

Thor's scowl was a fearsome thing. He pushed open the door, plowed through the photographers, and got me inside without incident.

I took a breath, then made my way to the reception desk. "Do you have any messages for me?"

"This was left for you, Mademoiselle Fields." A young man handed me an envelope.

"*Merci.*" I slit the heavy paper and pulled out the handwritten note—Ghislain Lambert hoped to see me and Chariss at his party. He lived on Quai Henri IV.

Thor didn't approve of lingering in the lobby. "Let's go." He planted his hand in the small of my back and propelled me forward. Propelled me into a stranger.

Of course, I tripped. Of course, I fell. Of course, I took the stranger with me.

I landed on top of him, his nose mere millimeters from mine. His eyes, surprised, wide, and the exact shade of Baltic amber, looked into mine.

"What the hell?" The stranger pushed me away.

"I'm so sorry." I struggled to my feet, twisted an ankle, and cartwheeled my arms for balance. The Hermès bag whacked the stranger in the head and he went down a second time.

"Oh! Oh my gosh!" I knelt next to him. "Are you all right?"

He said something unintelligible, then looked into my eyes a second time and stopped talking.

Now that we weren't so close, I could see him too. Maybe thirty. Not handsome. Not at all. But interesting. Even compelling. I freed my arm from the Hermès bag and pressed my hands against my galloping heart. "Are you all right?" I asked a second time. Maybe he didn't speak English. "*Ça va? Est-ce que je vous ai blessé? Je suis désolée.*"

He rubbed his jaw. "I'm fine." Russian. The man was Russian. I could tell from his accent.

Thor grabbed my arm and hauled me off the floor. "Are you hurt?" he demanded in a tone that suggested protecting me should qualify him for hazard pay. Given our morning, it probably should.

I shook him off and extended my hand to the Russian still on the floor. "Again, I am so, so sorry."

The Russian's fingers closed around my hand. He pulled

himself to standing, glanced at Thor, then returned his gaze to me. "You can make it up to me. Have a drink with me."

Thor made a sound like teeth grinding.

I glanced back at him. The reason he sounded as if he were grinding his teeth was because he was.

If I were a man, I wouldn't appreciate some Russian who oozed sex appeal hitting on the girl I was with. True, Thor and I weren't together—but the Russian didn't know that.

The Russian still held onto my fingers. He squeezed them, reclaiming my attention. "I'm Viktor Prokorhov."

"Poppy Fields." I tugged gently on my hand. "Now's not the best time for a drink."

Viktor didn't let go. "You're staying at the Ritz?"

"I am." I tugged again.

"Then we will have a drink another time. Tonight," Viktor declared.

"We'll see." My life was complicated enough without adding a Russian to the mix. "I'm sorry I knocked you down."

"I'm not." Again he stared into my eyes.

A flush warmed my toes and climbed to my cheeks.

Thor's fingers pressed against the small of my back. This time when he pushed, I didn't stumble.

We boarded the elevator and when the doors slid closed, Thor scowled at me. "Do you have any idea who that was?"

"He said his name was Viktor Prokorhov."

"And his father is Yurgi Prokorhov."

I waited for more.

"He's a Russian oligarch." Thor's tone told me I should know who Yurgi was. I didn't.

"Is he the one in Chariss's suite?"

Thor's brows met over his nose. "What?"

"There's a Russian oligarch in the Imperial suite. Chariss's favorite. She's in the Coco Chanel suite instead. She's not exactly happy about it."

The elevator doors slid open. Thor stepped out into the hallway and looked both ways. "I don't know about your mother's suite, but I do know Prokorhov runs the largest bank in Russia. He owns mines. He owns newspapers."

I followed him into the corridor. "Why are you telling me this?"

"Prokorhov is a bad guy."

"How do you know?"

"I just do. If you tell Brown about this, he'll ask you to get close to Viktor."

There were worse fates. "I thought Mr. Brown only cared about shutting down the flow of illegal drugs." I waited as Thor opened the door to the suite and scanned the suite.

He waved me inside.

I dropped the orange Hermès shopping bag onto the sofa. "Are you saying there's more to Mr. Brown than he lets on?"

"I'm not saying anything. If Mr. Brown wants you to know something, he'll tell you."

"Sharing information isn't exactly his thing."

Thor actually smiled. That smile changed everything about him. He transformed from a handsome but dour Norse god into someone real. Someone even better-looking than Chris Hemsworth. I joined the Hermès bag on the couch.

"What's wrong?" he asked.

"Nothing." I wasn't remotely affected by the handsome Norse god who'd saved my life earlier today. I was not.

Especially not when he pulled his phone out his pocket, glanced at the screen, and scowled. "Speak of the devil."

"It's Mr. Brown?"

He nodded once, pushed a button, put the phone to his ear, and turned away from me.

Obviously, he wanted privacy. Obviously, they were talking about me. I didn't move. Instead I reached for the Hermès bag.

Admittedly, the tissue crinkled when I removed my new

handbag from the shopping bag, but that tiny bit of noise couldn't possibly justify the ferocious scowl Thor gave me.

I smiled sweetly and listened hard.

"But—" Whatever Mr. Brown was saying, Thor did not agree.

I listened harder.

"It's too dangerous, sir." Thor glanced my way.

I restrained, barely, from sticking my tongue out at him.

Thor remained silent, but his expression soured with each passing second. Soured until he looked as if he'd been sucking lemons.

They were definitely talking about me. "Sir—"

I had to say something. "I'm not without skills."

Thor rolled his eyes.

I stood and glared at him. "What are you talking about?"

"Do you mind?" A second passed. "No, sir, I wasn't speaking to you. Miss Fields was inquiring about our conversation." Another second passed then, impossibly, the expression on Thor's face soured even more. He held his phone out to me.

I took it. "Hello."

"Miss Fields." Mr. Brown's even tone was at odds with Thor's expression.

"Hello, sir." I took a deep breath. "What's up?"

"We have a plan in place. All you need to do is enter some details into the calendar on your phone."

I glanced at Thor. "No problem."

"This could be risky."

Another deep breath. "Like I said, no problem."

"Good. Tomorrow night. Nine o'clock. At Le Squelette. It's a café in the Latin Quarter. Got that?"

I repeated back the place and time. "Why would I go there?"

"Why wouldn't you?"

"The Latin Quarter isn't exactly a destination spot for me."

Situated on the Left Bank, it was a great place for inexpensive lunches, cheap bottles of beer, and getting lost on the maze-like streets. "Won't they guess this is a trap?" Whoever *they* were would surely know a woman who skipped lines at Triomphe wouldn't set a rendezvous in a bar called The Skeleton.

Mr. Brown grunted. "Just make a note that you're meeting a man."

"But—" I had serious reservations about this plan.

"Miss Fields, we've gone to a great deal of trouble to put this together. Please, just do as I ask."

I said nothing else. My mistake.

SIX

Ghislain Lambert lived on the Quai Henri IV on the top two floors of a building overlooking the Seine. He had a spectacular terrace and an even more spectacular view to go with it. Thor and I stood side by side next to the railing and gazed out at the city.

The memory of mist weighted the air. Rain might start again soon, but, for now, the night sparkled with possibility.

Below us, on the river, a bateau mouche glided past Ile St. Louis.

To our right, the bell towers and steeple of Notre Dame rose above the other buildings on Ile de la Cité.

A Madeleine Peyroux song floated through the open doors of the apartment. "Careless Love" slow-danced across the veranda.

The darkness around us was soft as cashmere and colored a deep indigo. The light on the water was golden.

It was all almost too romantic. My thoughts wandered to Jake. He would love this place. This night.

My hands tightened on the damp railing. Thinking of Jake —Jake, himself—brought me nothing but trouble. Thor and I had a job to do. I should focus on that. "Private banking can't possibly pay for this," I murmured.

"How much does a place like this cost?" Thor stood a couple of feet away from me, but his voice borrowed from the velvet mist—it wrapped around me.

"Several million." Why was I breathless?

Thor inched away from me. "Shouldn't you be talking to Lambert?"

"It's better if he comes looking for me."

"He might not know you're here."

"He knows."

Thor crossed his arms "How can you be so sure?"

"I just am." Our arrival had caused a stir. I touched the locket at my neck—a talisman. I'd lost it once. Never again.

"You should look for him," Thor insisted.

"If I didn't know better, I'd think you're trying to get rid of me."

The Norse god next to me stiffened.

"Trust me. It's better if he finds me with you."

"With me? Why?"

"Because he'll make assumptions."

"He'll think we're together." Thor put a few more inches between us.

"Exactly. Men like Lambert…" I searched for the best explanation. "If he thinks I'm a challenge, he'll be more interested. It's about the chase."

"And you don't care?"

"I don't. People have been making assumptions about me since the day I moved in with Chariss." I looked out over the Seine. "Lambert assumes I'm a prize to be won."

Thor's hands tightened around the railing. "Fine, we'll do it your way."

I turned away from the view and studied my bodyguard. "Are you feeling all right?"

"What? Yes." His brow wrinkled. "Why?"

"That was almost painless."

He snorted. "I already figured out telling to do you things doesn't work."

That made him smarter than almost every man I'd ever met.

I sighed and pulled away from the rail.

He caught my wrist. "You're not mad?"

"Not remotely." My face felt tight. I relaxed my jaw. "It's been a rough day."

"Yeah."

Something in his voice stopped me—made me look at him closely.

"If killing someone doesn't bother you, there's something wrong with you."

What bothered me more than killing the man at Antoine's was the empty place where guilt should be. The man I'd killed wanted to kidnap me. He'd held a gun to Gaston's head. He'd almost killed Thor. Those truths eclipsed the fact that he'd been someone's son—maybe husband, maybe father. Maybe something was wrong with me.

"Does it always bother you?" I asked. "Killing people?"

"Always." He stared out at the river. "Getting desensitized to violence is the worst thing that can happen to a soul."

Thor had unexpected depths. Attractive depths.

"Thank you," I said. "For this morning. For killing those men to protect me."

"I should be thanking you." He didn't sound even a little bit grateful.

"Let's call it even. I'll go find Lambert." I left him on the terrace before I said something I'd regret.

Inside, the table lamps were turned down low enough for the lights of Paris to pour inside. Effortlessly stylish women and men with great hair chatted and smoked and looked altogether *bon chic, bon genre* (well-educated, well-connected, and probably descended from France's aristocratic families).

The salon was dotted with clusters of delicate fauteuils and glass tables. The walls were covered with modern art.

I made my way toward the bar in the far corner.

"You said you'd have a drink with me. How about now?"

I looked up at Viktor Prokorhov. Curse the luck. Not that being pursued by the handsome son of a billionaire was a bad thing...but I had things to do. "And I will. Are you here for a while?"

"I am now." Those amber eyes of his were almost hypnotic.

"There's someone I must speak with, but I'll find you." I slipped away before he said something charming and tempted me to linger.

The weight of his gaze settled across my back and shoulders. Where was Lambert? I poked my head into a smaller salon and disturbed a man (did every man in Paris have great hair?) bent over a glass coffee table with a razor and a mound of white powder.

"Sorry." I backed out of the room.

"*Vous pouvez me rejoindre.*" He regarded me with glittering eyes.

"No, thanks." Coke was not my thing.

I hurried down the hallway to a stairway.

It would be rude to climb those stairs. I did it anyway.

Halfway to the top, I heard Ghislain Lambert's voice and my steps slowed.

He sounded angry. His words came in staccato beats.

My steps stopped, and I listened hard.

Ghislain was speaking a language I didn't understand, but he was talking about Paris. I recognized "*Gare du Nord,*" and "*Pompidou*" and "*Les Deux Magots*" and "*Le Tour Eiffel.*"

The voices (Lambert's and a woman's) grew louder. Almost as if they were walking toward the stairs.

Zut!

I reversed. Racing down the steps I'd just climbed, I dashed into the nearest room and eased the door shut. My heart thumped in my ears and I leaned heavily against the door's solid expanse. Maybe I wasn't cut out for spying.

The clack of a woman's heels on the chevron parquet and the heavier tread of a man's shoes breached the door.

When they'd passed, I cracked the door and stared after them. Lambert had his hand on the woman's elbow. Straight dark hair brushed her shoulders and her dress was black. From the back, she looked like seventy percent of the women at the party—right down to the red heels of her shoes.

Ignoring a chilling, plunged-in-ice-water sensation, I tiptoed after them.

I reached the main salon too late. Ghislain Lambert stood by himself. And I'd been right about it being difficult to identify the woman—there were at least fifteen brunettes wearing black dresses.

Being a spy was way harder than it looked in the movies.

I eased into the room, scanning the women's faces, searching for one who looked as if she'd just had an argument with her host. They all looked sanguine. Not a single one looked remotely upset or out of sorts.

"You came."

I jumped, then manufactured a smile. "I said I would."

Ghislain Lambert smiled back. "You look beautiful."

"Thank you." I glanced around the salon. "Your home is breathtaking."

"Sadly, it's not mine. A friend is living in Singapore for a year and he invited me to stay here."

"How lucky for you."

"Yes." He patted his jacket and took out a pack of cigarettes. "Cigarette?"

"No, thank you."

"Do you mind if I smoke?"

Yes. "Of course not."

He lit a cigarette. "What may I get you from the bar?"

"Kir."

His eyes twinkled. "I thought Americans drank only cocktails."

"Sometimes."

He smiled as if I'd said something clever. "Don't move. I'll be right back."

Ghislain walked to the bar without looking at a single brunette.

This job would be much easier if I knew what I was listening for or who I was supposed to watch.

A Juliette Armanet song filtered through the chatter. Somehow both sexy and sad, the song was very, very French. Leave it to a Frenchwoman to make loneliness sound good. Loneliness wasn't beautiful or romantic. Not remotely. I knew firsthand. When I'd thought Jake was dead, loneliness nearly crushed me.

"You look a million miles away."

"Do I?" I must have been more than a million miles away to let Viktor sneak up on me.

Viktor nodded. "It is time for our drink?"

"Our host is at the bar getting me a drink right now."

"You know Ghislain?"

This was Ghislain's party. "I met him last night. You?"

"He does business with my father."

Now, that was interesting.

"Your kir." Ghislain presented me with a glass of crème-de-cassis-laced wine.

"*Merci*."

"You've met Viktor." Ghislain didn't sound all that pleased.

"I knocked him down earlier today." I took a tiny sip of my drink. "Twice."

"We're both staying at the Ritz." Viktor smiled at me as if

my whacking him in the head was the highlight of his trip to Paris. "Poppy knows how to make an entrance."

Ghislain's brows rose. "I have no doubt."

"I accidentally hit him in the head with my shopping bag."

"And you knocked him down? What did you buy?"

"An Hermès bag."

Ghislain choked on a laugh. "I thought you were made of tougher stuff, Viktor. Does Yurgi know?"

The Russian's brows lowered and violence seemed to shimmer on his skin.

It was time to change the subject. I cast about for something to say. "What brings you to Paris, Viktor?"

"Business." There was something almost feral about Viktor's smile and I was reminded of what Thor had said about Viktor's father—that he was a bad man. "And you?"

"My mother is shooting a movie. She asked me to come and keep her company."

"Are you here long?" asked Ghislain.

"I haven't decided." I glanced around the salon. I was never going to figure out which woman had been talking with Ghislain. "You know—" I rested a hand on my host's arm "—I'd love a tour of this place."

"It would be my pleasure. Viktor, do you want to join us?" Ghislain's words were welcoming but his eyes said *I'll cut you with a knife.*

"Please." Apparently, the Russian wasn't too worried about annoying a Frenchman.

"Is DuChamp here?" Ghislain scanned the salon. "Maybe he'd like to join us."

"If he was here, he'd love it. Unfortunately, he couldn't come tonight."

"What a pity." Ghislain didn't sound remotely sorry André hadn't come.

"He took Dylan Roberts on a tour of the catacombs."

The sneer that flashed across Ghislain's face exactly reflected my feelings on André's choice. "You came alone?"

"Not exactly. My bodyguard is here. I hope you don't mind." Now I scanned the room. "He's over by the door."

Both Ghislain and Viktor shifted their gazes to Thor, who wore a thunderous expression, as if Odin had just taken away his hammer.

"He certainly brings life and gaiety to a party," observed Ghislain. Apparently having a saturnine Norse god guard the exit to the terrace hadn't factored into his party planning. Men were actually skirting Thor to get outside. Not so much the women—a surly man who looked like Chris Hemsworth still looked like Chris Hemsworth.

"I saw you with him at the hotel," observed Viktor. "I wondered who he was."

"Why do you need a bodyguard?" Ghislain was still staring at Thor as if the weight of his stare could somehow remove him from the apartment. "You didn't have one at the club."

"There have been threats."

"Threats?" asked Viktor.

"An attempt," I admitted.

"An attempt? On your life?" Ghislain's brows rose.

"Last night." If they wanted to know more, they could google me. "I feel safer with him around." The truth in that statement made me blink. "He's very—" I searched for the right word—brave, cranky, handsome, bossy "—capable. If you're sure none of your guests will try to kill me, he can guard the door during our tour."

"No one would dare lift a finger against you in my home."

"And if they do—" a wolfish grin lit Viktor's face "—I'll protect you."

Mentioning that I'd taken him down with a shopping bag would be rude.

Ghislain did it anyway. "Didn't she knock you flat?"

Viktor's grin faltered but held firm. "Yes, but tonight she is without her shopping bag."

Ghislain tipped his head to the side, pursed his lips, and lifted his hands in the air. "*Bof.*" He'd managed a Gallic shrug without moving his shoulders. Even without the shoulders, Ghislain's shrug clearly suggested a mild breeze could knock Viktor down.

"I caught Viktor by surprise." I wasn't helping. Viktor's jaw was working as if his temper was tugging on its leash.

Ghislain didn't seem to notice that Viktor wanted to knock him flat. He waved his hand at the room filled with chattering people. "You've seen the grand salon. This way to the dining room."

The dining table, a sheet of heavy glass balanced on Rococo pedestals, was covered with a cheese tray, baskets of bread and crackers, and a large bowl of spiced nuts. Party food by a bachelor. The windows, flanked by curtains in that shade of goldenrod yellow so many Parisians favored, opened onto the terrace and a view of the Seine.

"Lovely." I picked up the silver spoon and dropped a few nuts into my palm.

"The kitchen is through there."

"Do you cook?" I asked.

"I make a delicious *petit déjeuner*. Omelets and coffee and pastry from the patisserie around the corner. Perhaps you will join me someday?"

I pretended not to understand the implication. "I'm not much a breakfast eater."

A smile touched Viktor's lips.

They were competing for a prize they couldn't win.

There ought to be a way to easily communicate intentions. A symbol that said *not available for one-night stands and not interested in getting involved*. If there was, I'd have a pendant made and wear it all the time. My hand rose to the locket at my neck. "What kind of business do you do together?"

Ghislain tilted his head. "Pardon me?"

"You and Viktor and his father. What kind of business do you do together?"

A shadow glided across Ghislain's face. "Banking, of course." Liar, liar.

"Of course."

"This way." Ghislain led us down the hallway to the salon where I'd seen the man cutting coke. The room was empty now. "My library."

I stepped inside and turned back toward the door. Built-in bookshelves covered the wall. I scanned the titles and saw everything from Proust to Phillipe Labro.

"You enjoy books?" asked Ghislain.

"Very much."

I touched the spine of *Du côté de chez Swann*.

"You've read Proust?" Patronizing me wasn't the best way to get on my good side.

"No." On purpose.

Ghislain kissed the tips of his fingers. "A man's search for meaning in a world that seems meaningless."

Way too heavy for my tastes.

"What do you read?" asked Viktor.

If he was hoping I'd say Tolstoy or Chekhov, he was destined for disappointment. "I read hopeful books. Broken relationships mended. Murderers caught. Evildoers punished."

"Fairy tales," said Ghislain.

"Fantasy," said Viktor.

"Let's see the rest of the apartment," said I.

The stairs I'd almost climbed led to a large open area with a view of the building's courtyard. The rest of the floor was taken up with bedrooms and Ghislain's study (glass desk, two computer monitors, a view of the Seine).

"Poppy."

I turned and spotted Thor in the doorway. "Yes?"

"We should go."

"Oh?"

"Someone tagged you."

"What?"

"Someone took a picture of you with their location. This location."

I knew what tagging was. I was the one who'd explained it to him "So?"

"Given last night's attempt, you'd be safer elsewhere."

"Who did this?" demanded Ghislain.

Thor glanced down at his phone. "Elisabeth Verdurin."

Ghislain blinked a few times, then raked his fingers through his hair. "I'm sorry your privacy was invaded—your safety compromised."

"It's not your fault. Besides, it happens all the time." The invasion of privacy part—and, lately, the safety part, more often than I cared to admit.

"Still, it happened at my house." Ghislain clenched his hands into fists. The cool Parisian was ready to march downstairs and wring the woman's neck.

I touched his arm. "That woman—Elisabeth—she had no idea posting would be dangerous for me."

A muscle in Ghislain's cheek twitched. Elisabeth Verdurin wouldn't be invited to any more parties at this borrowed apartment.

"My car and driver are around the corner," said Viktor. "It would be an honor to return you safely to the Ritz."

That muscle in Ghislain's cheek twitched double time.

I looked at Thor and raised my brows.

He answered with a small nod.

"Thank you, Viktor. We'd appreciate that."

"If you'll call your driver, Mr. Prokorhov, I'll check the lobby." Thor's expression was serious. Focused in a way that made me worry. "I'll call Miss Fields when everything's clear."

"Fine." Viktor pulled his phone out of his pocket.

Thor disappeared.

Ghislain scowled.

I looked out the window at the city bathed in golden light and wondered if we'd make it back to the hotel.

SEVEN

Viktor's driver pulled up in front of Ghislain's apartment building in a tank. A Mercedes, glossy black and ridiculously luxurious, but still a tank. It was one of those enormous cars favored by third-world dictators and…and Russian oligarchs.

The uniformed driver looked like Arnold Schwarzenegger back when he was playing barbarians. But bigger. He opened the back door with a hand the size of a dinner plate and Thor bundled me inside. Viktor climbed in behind me.

Thor took the front passenger seat and the driver pulled into traffic on the Quai Henri IV.

On our right, the Seine flowed in black and gold ribbons.

I leaned my head back and closed my eyes. We were fine. Thor was just nervous because of what had happened at Antoine's. We were fine. If I kept repeating that, it would be true.

Thunk!

I looked over my shoulder. "Wha—"

"Get down!" Thor held a gun in his hand.

Viktor grabbed my wrist and pulled me off the seat and onto the floorboards.

Thunk, thunk, thunk!

"Bulletproof glass," said the driver as he swerved around a slow-moving car.

I lifted my head high enough to see out the window.

"Stay down!" Thor barked.

"Bulletproof glass," I barked back. Besides, I was a government agent. Government agents didn't cower on the floorboards when they were attacked. They grabbed a gun and shot back.

I didn't have a gun.

Gun or no, I wouldn't cower. I lifted my head and glanced through the windshield.

Viktor's driver yanked the wheel to the right, missing a Mini by only an inch or two.

I raised my head a little higher and looked through the rear window.

A car every bit as enormous as Viktor's clipped the Mini. The little car spun in a circle and crashed into a streetlight.

The big car kept coming.

"Get down!" yelled Thor.

"You're very bossy."

"It's my job to keep you alive." Thor sounded as if he were reconsidering his career choices.

Thunk, thunk, thunk!

More bullets.

"Why do they keep shooting?"

"Because sometimes, if the gun is big enough, the glass breaks."

So, only bulletproof to a point. Good to know. I lowered my head.

Thor leaned over the backseat and glowered at me. "Stay down." He glanced out the back window and his jaw slackened. "Turn. Now!"

The car careened and Viktor tumbled onto me.

The light outside the car went from gold to orange and the car shuddered.

I lifted my head and peeked. I had to. We were crossing the Seine. Behind us a cluster of destroyed trees were on fire. Ahead of us lay Les Jardins des Plantes. That meant we were on the Pont d'Austerlitz.

"Right!" Thor shouted.

The driver completed another gut-wrenching turn and the Seine was on our right again.

The car flew down Quai Saint-Bernard, weaving between cars, honking, and even nudging a slow-moving vehicle with its front bumper.

The other car was still behind us.

Viktor was still half on top of me.

"What did they shoot at us? I demanded.

Thor didn't answer me. Instead, he spoke to the driver. "Can this car go any faster?"The driver took Thor's question as an invitation to floor the accelerator. The car shot forward.

I pushed Viktor off of my chest.

The driver swerved and Viktor fell on me again. His elbow landed in my gut.

"*Ooof!*"

"Stay down," Thor growled. "Please."

Thunk, thunk, thunk!

"*Putain de merde.*" The driver had a way with words.

I didn't bother pushing on Viktor, he'd just fall on me again.

"Where are we going?" I was proud my voice didn't waver. "What's your plan?"

"My plan?" Thor replied.

Of course he had a plan. He had to have a plan.

Thunk, thunk, thunk!

The driver swerved right. The car popped a curb. And we sped forward at an angle.

Outside, someone shrieked, and I imagined some poor woman out for a late evening promenade diving out of the way.

The driver glanced over his shoulder. *"Merde."*

Hopefully that didn't mean the screaming woman was shot or run over or dead in the street. "Can we get to the American embassy?" I squeaked.

Thunk, thunk, thunk.

"Or the Russian embassy." Viktor's squeak was higher.

"Where's a police station?" I demanded.

"Quiet!" Thor yelled.

"He's very bossy," I told Viktor.

"Dammit, Poppy. Stay down and shut up."

Rude!

The driver swerved left.

Viktor's elbow pushed every last bit of air out of my body and I gasped.

At least all four tires were on the pavement again.

Car chases in the movies looked exciting. Guns and the crunch of metal and high-octane speed.

We had all those things, but exciting wasn't the word I'd use to describe the experience. Sickening was a much better word. The few nuts I'd eaten at Ghislain's gurgled in my stomach. It would be better if I could see what was happening.

Thor put down his gun and put his phone to his ear. "We're in trouble. We're on the Left Bank next to the Seine."

I peeked out the window. "We're just passing Place Maubert."

"Get down!" Thor barked. "Did you hear that, sir?"

He listened for a few seconds.

"No, sir. This doesn't feel like a kidnapping attempt. This feels like an assassination attempt." He listened for a few more seconds, dropped the phone into his lap, and picked up his gun.

"What's happening?" I demanded.

He leaned over the seat and looked down at me. "Help is coming. We just need to hold out for a few more minu—" He glanced out the rear window and his eyes widened. "Get down."

I couldn't go any lower.

Boom!

The car shuddered, the rear end lifted off the pavement, and a blast of heat washed over us.

My heart relocated to my throat.

The car's back wheels slammed onto the pavement with bone-jarring impact.

The driver let loose a stream of curses that would do a sailor in Marseilles proud.

Viktor whimpered.

We skidded to a stop.

"Are you hurt? Are you?"

It took a few seconds to realize Thor was yelling at me.

"I'm fine." If shaking and terrified and angry counted as fine, I was definitely fine.

"C'mon." He jerked his head toward the door. "We need to move. Now."

Gunfire erupted outside the car.

I lifted myself off the floorboards and peeked out the window.

The men in the car behind us weren't shooting at us. They were shooting at someone else. Someone behind them.

"C'mon!" Thor wasn't wasting the opportunity for escape.

I crawled over Viktor, who seemed almost catatonic, and opened the door. "Are you coming?"

The Russian didn't move—didn't answer.

Thor's hand braceleted my wrist and he pulled me out of the car. "We need to move. Now. Run."

"No. We can't just leave him." With my free arm, I tugged at Viktor. Adrenaline gave me unexpected strength and I pulled his torso free of the car.

Viktor's eyes fluttered open. "They're after you?"

"Yes!" Thor pulled at me. "Poppy, c'mon."

I resisted. "We have to get Viktor out of the car. What if it explodes?"

"Go. Nicolas will protect me."

The driver, holding an enormous gun and looking more barbarian-like than ever, had crawled out of the car and stood in the street looking for someone to shoot.

"C'mon." Thor pulled me toward the winding roads of the Latin Quarter.

Still, I resisted. "No."

"Fine." The look Thor gave me promised hell to pay, but he helped me pull Viktor free of the car. Together we half-walked/half-carried him to a recessed doorway.

"Are you all right?"

Viktor nodded. "Go."

I released my hold on him and, with one last look at the destroyed Mercedes, I let Thor pull me away.

We ran. Left, then right, then left again. We ran until we were hopelessly lost in the maze of the Latin Quarter. Cobble-stone streets too narrow for cars twisted every which way. Tiny ethnic restaurants and grocers nestled next to crêperies. An unlikely mix of scents—Chinese 5-spice and warm Nutella—filled my nose.

"Stop." There was a stitch in my side, I was gasping for breath, and my legs threatened complete collapse at any moment. Maybe Thor could run laps after a near-death experience, but I couldn't. "Please, stop."

He stopped, his face a mask of concern. "What? Are you okay? Where are you hurt?"

"I'm fine. We're running in circles."

"We are not."

"We are," I insisted. I pointed at a seedy café. "We've passed that café already."

"We have not."

"Yes—" I planted my hands on my hips "—we have." We totally had. "What are we doing?"

"Escaping."

"Really? Cause I thought we were running around." Not the nicest way to talk to a man who was trying to save me, but we'd been running in circles and I needed to sit. Preferably in a comfortable chair with my feet up and a glass of wine the size of a goldfish bowl in my hand.

Thor's answering scowl was thunderous. But, even with an expression that promised my impending doom fixed on his face, he scanned the people around us for threats.

"Look—" I tried for a reasonable tone "—we're only a few blocks from Boulevard St. Germain. We can get a taxi. You pick the destination. I'll go wherever you say and I won't argue."

"Fine." He turned his back on me and took a few steps.

"Mark."

My voice stopped him.

"Boulevard St. Germain is that way." I pointed the opposite direction.

He breathed fire through his nose.

Not really.

Almost.

He followed me to the corners of Boulevards St. Michel and St. Germain and waved down a taxi.

"*Où allez-vous?*" asked the driver.

I waited for Thor's answer, but my bodyguard was staring out the window.

"*The Ritz, s'il vous plaît.*"

The driver pulled into traffic.

"We can't go there," said Thor. "They could have someone waiting."

I desperately wanted to argue. Too bad I'd promised not to. Instead I said to the driver, "*Pardon, monsieur.*"

The driver looked at me in the rearview mirror. "*Oui?*"

"*S'il vous plait l'hôtel Shangri-La. Il est situé sur l'Avenue d'Iena.*"

"The Shangri-La?" asked Thor.

"It took four years to refurbish the Ritz."

"And?"

"When Chariss and I came to Paris when the Ritz was closed, we stayed at the Shangri-La. It's the first place that came to mind."

He nodded. Then, without another word, he turned in his seat and looked out the rear window.

"Are we being followed?" I whispered.

"No."

The night manager at the Shangri-La, Monsieur Guillaume, recognized me and emerged from behind the discreet reception desk. A furrow darkened his brow. "*Mademoiselle Fields, qu'est-ce qu'il passe? Ça va?*"

"*Ça va. Avez-vous une chambre?*" If the hotel was fully booked, I'd manufacture some tears. I *needed* rest. I *needed* a meal. I *needed* a drink.

"We have only the Suite Shangri-La."

"We'll take it." At that point, twenty thousand dollars for a place to rest seemed like a bargain. "Also, we'll need a bottle of wine, some sandwiches—you know the ones I like, and—" I looked at Thor and guessed "—a bottle of bourbon."

"Of course."

"May I fill out the registration in the morning? I'm dead on my feet." The hotel's tile floors seemed to be rising up through my heels. Parts of me I didn't know existed ached. Thor's hand on my elbow was the only things keeping me upright.

Monsieur Guillaume rubbed his chin. "I saw on the news that someone shot at you last night. Outside the Ritz." His tone suggested the Ritz was responsible.

I nodded. "I'd just as soon no one know I'm here until tomorrow."

"Zut." He shook his head sadly, a French reaction to the sorry state of a world where women were shot at in the first arrondissement. His expression said such things would not happen in the sixteenth. "Give me five minutes. *Cinq minutes.*"

Getting us checked in anonymously took him less than three minutes. He returned to where we waited in the elegant lobby and presented me with key cards. "We miss having you here. Tell your mother to return to us."

"I will." Because he had been so kind I added, "The Ritz has her in the wrong suite."

Monsieur Guillaume grinned. "That would never happen here."

"Thank you." My fingers tightened around the keys.

"Room service will arrive within a few minutes."

"*Merci.*"

Thor and I rode the elevator to the penthouse suite. A wall of windows offered the best views of the Eiffel Tower in all of Paris. With its lights on, it looked cast in gold.

"Wow," Thor murmured.

"I know, right?" I collapsed onto a velvet couch.

Thor opened the glass door and stepped out onto the deck.

I closed my eyes, flexed and released my toes, and concentrated on breathing. Each breath was reason for gratitude.

Thor's voice drifted through the open door.

"Major firepower, sir. They took out Yurgi Prokorhov's Mercedes."

There was a moment's silence.

"Viktor Prokorhov offered her a ride, sir."

More silence.

"She met him at the Ritz and he was at Lambert's party tonight."

I rubbed the back of my neck.

"I'm pretty sure it was a coincidence."

It was nice of Thor not to tell John Brown I'd knocked Viktor down.

"She's resting, sir."

It was too much effort to turn my head or open my eyes. There was no way I could talk to John Brown tonight.

Tap, tap.

"*Entrez*," I called. I opened my eyes, but otherwise didn't move.

Thor bounded inside from the terrace with one hand on his phone and the other on his gun.

The waiter, who was depositing a tray of sandwiches and two bottles on the dining table, almost dropped the bourbon. The Blanton's bottle slipped through his fingers, but he somehow caught the jockey-on-top cork.

"Apologize to the nice waiter."

The look Thor gave me would have turned most women to stone. I yawned.

"I'll call you back, sir." Thor thrust a handful of euro at the waiter. "Sorry about that."

The pale and shaking waiter accepted the bills and melted out of our suite.

There was food waiting for me. Only a few feet away. All I had to do was stand. But I lacked the strength.

"Can I get you something?" Thor slid his gun into its holster and walked over to the table

I could have kissed him. "There should be some ham and cheese sandwiches. One of those and a glass of wine, please."

He opened the wine, poured me a filled-to-the-brim glass, and brought me a sandwich.

I took a bite and moaned softly. "You should eat something."

He stood staring at me—still as a statue in the Louvre. "I will in a minute."

"You look as if you have important things to say." I spoke around a mouthful of ham and cheese.

He sat on the chair across from me. "We need to talk."

Nothing good ever came of that sentence. "Not now."

He leaned forward, planting his elbows on his knees. "It's important."

"I'm hungry." I held up my sandwich. "I need a drink." I held up my half-full wine glass. "And I don't want to think about anything more serious than the temperature of my bath."

He blinked. "Your bath?"

"My bath. That's what I'm doing as soon as I find the energy to get off this couch."

"We need to talk."

"You already said that."

"You're in danger."

"I was in danger before."

"This was a bold attack."

"Bof." I gave him my best impression of a Gallic shrug.

There was that thunderous scowl I was coming to know so well. "I'm serious."

I was too. I took a giant sip of wine. "We're safe right now. I'll worry about being in danger in the morning."

"But—"

"We both need to recharge. If I was wrong about the bourbon, order whatever you want." Clutching my sandwich and my wine, I hauled myself off the couch and stumbled toward one of the bedrooms. I reached the door and looked back at Thor. "Thank you."

"For what?"

"For protecting me." Then, before he could say something stupid like *it's my job,* I slipped into the bedroom and closed the door.

EIGHT

Thor found me stretched out on a cloud-like chaise on the suite's terrace. Across from where I lounged, the Eiffel Tower pressed against an impossibly blue sky. Birds sang. Paris smelled sweet.

On the table next to me was a pot of coffee, a basket of croissants, fresh butter, and to-die-for orange marmalade.

Staying where I was—forever—seemed like a good plan.

Thor lowered himself onto a chair. Slowly. As if he too was feeling the effects of last night's chase. Or maybe he'd put a dent in the bourbon. "You look better this morning."

I took a sip of coffee and stretched in the morning sunshine. "I feel better."

"We need to talk."

Again with the *we need to talk*. "Eat something first. The croissants are still warm."

The corner of his eye twitched, but he poured himself a cup of coffee and gazed at the Eiffel Tower.

"Relax. Just for a few minutes." I was. Chances were excellent these moments on the terrace would be the best part of my day. I was going to enjoy each one.

Thor's eye twitched again and he opened his mouth as if to say something I didn't want to hear.

I held up my hand, stopping whatever dire words were on his tongue. "Relax."

"You're avoiding talking about what happened last night."

"No, I'm not." Yes, I was.

And who could blame me? The sun was warm on my face, I'd slept in a dream of a bed, and Paris looked beautiful. Why spoil the morning with talk of violence and death?

"We have to talk." He wasn't giving up.

I sighed. "Did Viktor make it back to the Ritz safely?"

"That's your question?" There was a sharp edge to his voice. The man really ought to put his feet up.

"That's one of my questions. I'd also like to know who was shooting at the people who blew up Viktor's car."

"You don't wonder who might want you dead?"

"That I know." I stretched again, reaching my arms toward the sky. "There's only one person."

"Javier Diaz. Doesn't that worry you?"

"Of course it does." I dropped one of my hands to the locket at my neck. "What I don't get is why he didn't have me killed in California. There were days when I walked on the beach with no one for company but—" my heart constricted "—Consuela." I patted the pockets of my robe. Empty. Then I remembered I'd left my dead cell in the bedroom. "We need to call the Ritz. Right away."

"Why? What's wrong?"

"May I borrow your phone? Please? I need to check on Consuela. Chariss won't take care of her. She just won't. She won't take her for a walk. She won't feed her breakfast. She won't—"

Thor handed me his cell. "Someone from the hotel will do all that?"

"Of course. The maids love her." A stretch. Consuela was

a one-person dog and treated the staff at the Ritz with disdain. "They took her out last night because I was worried we'd be late." I drummed my fingertips against my lower lip until someone answered. "*Bonjour*—" I made my request, listened to the concierge's answer "—*merci.*" I hung up. "That's settled. One of the maids Consuela likes—" tolerates "—will take care of her until we get back."

His eye twitched a third time. "You're more concerned about your dog than being shot at."

I took a sip of coffee rather than reply.

"About tonight—"

"It's a stupid plan."

"I agree."

I blinked back my surprise. "No one will believe I'm meeting someone in the Latin Quarter. I tried explaining that to Mr. Brown, but he wouldn't listen." I stared at Thor over the rim of my cup. "You've spent the past twenty-four hours with me. Is there anything in any of those minutes to suggest I'd schedule a rendezvous there?"

"You did know how to get us out of there."

"That?" I shook my head. "My mother dated a French director and she filmed more movies in Paris than I can count. When I was a teenager and I wasn't in school, I was in France —usually in Paris. While she worked, I roamed the city." I reached for a second croissant. "I've been lost in the Latin Quarter before."

"Your reason for thinking the plan is stupid is because you're too ritzy to hang out on the left bank?" His eye twitched like crazy.

"What's wrong with your eye?"

He glowered his response.

I studied the view. "It's not much of a trap if the people we're trying to trap are suspicious." Thor wasn't the only one who could glower. I could glower too. I glowered at him now. "They might turn the tables on us. And, for the record, I'm not ritzy. I just don't hang out in the Latin Quarter. It's crowded. The streets are a maze. And the shopping isn't very good."

Thor's gaze fixed on Monsieur Eiffel's marvel—almost as if he was avoiding my glower. "You wouldn't last a day in the Paris I know."

"Hmmph."

"Your Paris is chic nightclubs and elegant hotels and over-priced handbags. My Paris is seedy cafés and deals made in back alleys."

Surely he couldn't be referring to the bag André bought for me. "That handbag wasn't overpriced. It was made by a master craftsman."

"No one needs a ten-thousand-dollar handbag."

"Careful, Mark. You're giving me the impression you don't approve."

"This is more than anyone needs." He waved at the suite behind us.

"It was the only room they had. Besides the croissants are excellent—" I pushed the basket closer to him (I didn't need a third pastry) "—and you can't beat the view." I pointed at the Eiffel Tower. "As for surviving in Pigalle, I might surprise you."

Thor snorted, but he reached for a croissant.

"Who was shooting?" I asked.

"When?" A fair question. There'd been a lot of shooting lately.

"Who was shooting at the car that chased us?"

"I don't know."

"Was Jake following us?" Jake was the only person I could think of who'd willingly take on an opponent armed with a grenade launcher.

"Jake?" Thor took a bite of croissant.

"Yes. Jake. Tall. Sandy blond hair. Laugh lines."

"Don't know him."

"We all work for Mr. Brown." That was a pretty good hint.

"Still don't know him."

"Fine," I didn't believe him. I rose from my chair and tightened the belt of my robe. "We should probably head back to the Ritz." Consuela needed me.

"You're safer here." It was almost as if the view, and the croissants, and the excellent coffee were wearing Thor down. That or the gentle breeze ruffling his hair.

"My dog is at the Ritz."

"The maid is taking care of your dog."

"Ghislain Lambert will be calling."

"How do you know?"

"I just know." I glanced down at the folded copy of *Le Figaro*. I'd made the front page. Someone with a camera had captured an image of me pulling Viktor out of the Mercedes. Ghislain would be calling. Soon. And Chariss would be pulling her hair out. "May I use your phone again, please?"

He handed over his phone.

I took a deep breath and dialed.

The call went directly to voicemail. "Chariss, it's Poppy. I'm fine. I'll be back at the hotel soon. Bye." I returned the phone to him.

"Have you always called your mother Chariss?"

"When Chariss got the call that a pilot she'd made was being picked up, she lied about her age and left me with my dad. When I moved in with her after Dad was killed, she had a problem. Either she gave birth at fifteen or she'd been shaving off a few years. Either way, she did not want me calling her Mom. Chariss was the best option."

"Which was it?"

"Shaving. She was nineteen when I was born." I grinned. "Don't tell anyone."

"Your secret is safe with me."

"It's not my secret." The breeze grabbed a few strands of my hair and I smoothed them back into the tangle on my head. "I'm going to grab a shower. I'll be ready in twenty minutes."

Thor, who'd crammed half a croissant in his mouth, merely nodded.

The ride back to the Ritz was uneventful. Uneventful was good.

"I can call and ask someone to open the door on the Rue Cambon for us." As suggestions went, it was a good one.

Thor shook his head. "We've got people watching Place Vendôme. We should be fine using the front entrance."

The driver pulled into Place Vendôme and I sank lower in my seat. Half the paparazzi in France were camped in front of the Ritz. Thor's people might save me from a gunshot, but they couldn't save me from fifty snapping Canons. "*N'arrête pas*," I told the driver.

"*Oui, mademoiselle.*"

No sunglasses, no way to hide my face, last night's dress. I was not getting out of that taxi. "*Galeries Lafayette, s'il vous plaît.*"

"I didn't realize." Thor scanned the crowd of photographers with a stunned expression. "We can go to the Rue Cambon."

"Too late now. They'll just run around the corner." I leaned my head against the seat. "And if you're seen with me, your picture will be plastered everywhere. Did you ever want to work undercover?"

Thor's lips thinned. "So we're going shopping?"

"No way am I showing up at the Ritz in last night's dress."

His upper lip quivered as if he were fighting a sneer. Or a smile. There was no telling which.

The driver pulled up in front of Galeries Lafayette's entrance and I slipped out of the car. Thor could pay the fare.

I hurried inside, waiting just inside the door for Thor.

"Let's be fast," I said when he joined me.

"I don't even know what we're doing."

"Shopping."

The man gawked. First at me. Then he tilted his head toward Galeries Lafayette's glass-domed ceiling and gawked at that. He gawked for all of five seconds, then dismissed floor after floor of beautiful clothes and accessories with a single jerk of his chin. "Seriously?"

"Lower your voice. People are staring." Truth—they could have been staring because he looked like Chris Hemsworth (made even sexier by morning-after stubble and mussed hair). "This way."

Fifteen minutes later, we'd ridden the escalator to a boutique that wasn't too busy, and I had on a new pair of black pants, a black T-shirt, black loafers, and a pale pink trench coat. I was also the owner of a pair of Dior sunglasses and a silk scarf which I used to cover my hair.

I folded my dress and dropped it in a shopping bag with last night's shoes. "It's up to you to get this back to the Ritz."

"Where will you be?"

"We're taking separate cabs."

"What? No!"

"Follow me. Watch me walk through the door. Then come in ten minutes later. I'll be in the suite. The alternative is appearing on the cover of *Paris Match* together." Probably an exaggeration. A small exaggeration.

Thor glowered. He did that a lot.

I dashed outside and hopped in a taxi. "*The Ritz, s'il vous plait.*"

If the driver was annoyed about a fare of less than a kilometer, he kept it to himself.

If he was annoyed when his automobile was swamped by photographers, he kept that to himself too.

I swiped my credit card, left him a generous tip, and waited for the doorman to wade through the sea of Canons and Nikons with lenses as long as the photographers' forearms.

When the car door opened, I sprung out. Keeping my head down, I pushed toward the door of the Ritz.

I didn't stop. Not till I reached the lobby. And even then, I barely slowed. I practically ran to the suite I shared with Chariss.

I took one second for a deep, centering breath, pushed open the door, and dashed inside.

Ooomph!

I'd run smack-dab into a barrel chest and a Charvet shirt. I pulled the sunglasses off my nose and looked up at a face I didn't know. "Who are you?"

Had I somehow entered the wrong suite? I glanced around.

White on white with shades of ecru and brown for contrast. And Chariss was curled up in the corner of one of the couches as if she were some rare and beautiful breed of cat. I was definitely in the right suite.

"You're here. Thank heavens you're all right." My mother rose in one graceful movement, floated over to me, and kissed my cheek. She even wrapped me in a hug. "I was so worried."

"I'm fine." I lowered my voice. "Who's your guest?"

Chariss freed me from her embrace and donned her brightest smile. "Poppy, this is Yurgi Prokorhov. Yurgi, please meet my daughter, Poppy."

Yurgi Prokorhov had no hair on his head, but his eyebrows more than made up for the lack. His dark eyes were shrewd. His mouth was full. He was Viktor in another thirty years.

I extended my hand. "We owe you a Mercedes."

"Not at all," he replied. Undoubtedly music to Chariss's ears.

"That's so nice of you."

He shook his head. "I saw the pictures in the papers. Men were shooting, but you did not run. You stayed to help my son."

"Anyone would have done the same."

He chuckled as if I'd said something amusing.

"Yurgi stopped by to check on you," Chariss cooed.

"I'm fine. Really. Your car saved our lives."

Yurgi rubbed his chin. "Then it was worth every ruble. Cars can be replaced. My son, women like you and your mother, you are all priceless."

"I'm so glad Viktor is all right."

Yurgi rubbed his chin. "Your mother has agreed the two of you will dine with me and Viktor tonight."

I shot Chariss a look. She knew better than to make plans for me.

"She says she must be at work before the sun rises tomorrow, so it will be an early dinner."

It had better be. I was supposed to be bait tonight. "Sounds delightful. I look forward to it."

Yurgi moved toward the door. "I am sure you are tired. I will leave you to rest." He bent and air-kissed the top of my hand. "Until tonight."

Chariss opened the door for him. When he was gone, she turned on me. The smile disappeared from her face and her tone turned shrill. "Where have you been?"

"I spent the night at another hotel."

"Where?"

"The Shangri-La. Monsieur Guillaume misses you."

For a brief second her expression softened. A very brief second. "What the hell is going on?"

"I wish I knew." Why had Diaz decided to have me killed now?

"Figure it out. Fast," she snapped. "Where's that bodyguard?"

"He'll be here any minute."

"What good is he if he's not with you?"

"I told him to come after me."

"Oh?" Her tone promised more yelling.

"He's not hard on the eyes."

She ceded my point with a quick bob of her chin. "What has that got to do with anything?"

"There are a million photographers outside the hotel."

She narrowed her eyes. "Where's this going?"

"Climbing out of a cab with a man who looks like Mark Stone would start a gossip feeding frenzy." I looked around the suite. "Where's Consuela?"

Chariss pursed her lips. "You're concerned about the dog?"

"Yes."

"A maid took her for a walk."

I nodded. "I need to plug my phone in. It's completely dead." I walked toward my bedroom.

"Is that why you didn't answer?"

My steps faltered. "You called?"

"Of course I called. A million times. I was going out of my mind with worry." Every so often, Chariss surprised me.

I looked over my shoulder. "I'm sorry. I should have called you last night. When we got to the Shangri-La, I just collapsed."

"And this morning?"

"I left you a message."

"That was a big of you." Her shoulders were stiff; the grace she'd exhibited for Yurgi was gone. "You should have kept calling until I answered." She grabbed her handbag off the sofa table and strode toward the door to the hallway. "I have to go to work. We'll talk about this later."

"About dinner tonight—"

She pointed her finger at me. "You're going to dinner. That man's car, which probably cost half a million dollars, was blown up. You're going to dinner."

"I'm going." I held up hands to stop the tirade I sensed was coming. "But I have plans afterward."

She stared at me as if I'd just spoken gibberish. "Plans?"

Apparently, she had understood. I nodded.

"Plans?" Her voice was higher and louder than strictly necessary. "Someone launched a grenade at the car you were riding in last night and tonight you have plans?"

"Thor will protect me."

"Thor? Who the hell is Thor?"

Tap, tap.

Chariss marched over to the door and yanked it open. "You!" She glared at Thor as if he was personally responsible for the attempt on my life. "Keep my daughter out of trouble. I'd like her alive for dinner tonight." Then, with an impressive swirl of her hem, she stormed into the hall and slammed the door.

Thor handed me the Galeries Lafayette bag with my dress, shoes, and evening bag inside. "She's scary when she's angry."

I nodded.

"John Brown's been trying to call you."

"My phone's dead. Has been all morning."

"You need to call him. He's getting...agitated. It's about tonight."

"About that."

"What?"

"Chariss made dinner plans for us."

"Oh?"

"With Yurgi and Viktor Prokorhov."

His scowl was back and deeper than ever. Apparently, he had opinions about my dining with a Russian oligarch. "Where?"

"I don't know."

Tap, tap.

I reached for the door handle, but Thor shouldered past

me. "I'll get that." He opened the door and Consuela dashed into the suite.

She ran right to me. "*Yip.*"

I picked her up and hugged her. "How's my sweet pup?"

She licked my nose.

At least there was one person around who wasn't mad at me.

NINE

I left Thor in the suite's living room. Consuela and I retreated to my bedroom, where I plugged in my cell.

Notifications of missed calls, missed texts, and voicemails scrolled across the screen—Chariss (she really had called—more than once), André, my friend Mia, my agent, an unknown number, and a slew of other friends. It would take the rest of the day to return them all.

I group texted André and Mia (I'm fine. Don't worry. TTYL), dropped the phone on the bed, and sat down with Consuela on my lap. "I missed you."

"*Yip.*" She'd missed me, too.

"This whole situation," I whispered. "What a mess."

"*Yip,*" she agreed—especially since she'd had to take her morning walk with a maid.

I snuggled her closer. "Javier wants me dead."

"*Grrr.*" Consuela had never liked Javier.

My new shoes weren't as comfortable as they should be. I kicked them off, leaned back against the pillows, and thought. Hard.

Javier's assassins had come close to killing me last night. "Tonight we're giving them another chance."

"*Grrrr.*" Consuela thought my going to the Latin Quarter was a monumentally stupid idea.

"But we have to stop them," I told her. "If we don't, I'll be looking over my shoulder forever."

She stared at me with bright button eyes—eyes that said I'd better not get myself killed. Or else.

I stroked her fur. Stopping the hitmen Javier Diaz had sent after me wouldn't stop the attempts on my life. To do that, we'd have to stop Javier.

I sighed. We'd try things Mr. Brown's way, but if the trap he'd set for tonight didn't work, I had a plan of my own.

The phone on the bed vibrated and I looked down at the screen. It was almost as if John Brown knew I was thinking about him.

I let the phone ring again before I answered. "Hello."

"Stone says you're unscathed."

"I suppose so."

"Did you learn anything at Lambert's?" No small talk for Mr. Brown.

"I overheard him talking in a language I didn't understand. He mentioned some Paris landmarks."

"Which ones?"

"The Eiffel Tower, Gare du Nord—" I closed my eyes. "The others escape me right now."

Mr. Brown's disappointment traveled through the telephone. "That's it?"

"Yes."

"Nothing about accounts?"

"I just met the man. When was the last time someone you barely know offered to share confidential, illegal client information with you?"

Mr. Brown ignored my question. "Keep trying."

"It would be easier if I knew what I was listening for."

Mr. Brown was silent for a few long seconds. "How much do you know about money laundering, Miss Fields?"

"Not much," I admitted.

"Sometimes large banks serve as hubs for smaller banks needing access to the global banking system. We're pretty good at watching large banks, but some of the smaller banks, especially foreign ones, slip under our radar. There're just too many of them. It's up to the larger banks to make sure the transfers they receive through those smaller banks are clean."

"Sometimes they don't always do that?"

"Bingo."

"On purpose?"

"That's debatable."

"So drug dealers can clean their money by depositing cash in a small bank in a country that doesn't play well with U.S. regulators?"

"Exactly. There are places in Asia and South America where it's nearly impossible to effectively police the banks."

Understanding was dawning. "You think Ghislain Lambert is helping to clean dirty money?"

"It's possible. Probable. There's been chatter about a banker in France."

"There are lots of bankers in France."

"We have good reason to believe it's Lambert. Do you know with whom he was talking?"

"A woman. Dark hair. Medium height. Thin."

"You just described half the women in France."

"I know." I should have done more to figure out who she was. "I never saw her face."

Mr. Brown sighed.

I wasn't exactly proving my worth. In fact, the opposite. I'd made my boss sigh with disappointment. "About tonight —" I began.

"Everything's in place."

"I'm not sure that—"

"Stone has the complete plan. He'll tell you what you need to know."

"But—"

"Stone tells me you're having dinner with the Prokorhovs."

Good news traveled fast.

"Yes."

"Excellent." Mr. Brown sounded marginally less disappointed in me. "We're interested in the Prokorhovs."

"Anything I should be aware of?"

"No. Just start a relationship. We'll let you know if we want anything."

"But—"

"Good luck tonight, Miss Fields."

The cell in my hand went dead.

"*Grrr.*" Consuela was right. Grrr.

"If he doesn't trust me enough to tell me what's happening, this is going to be a short relationship."

"*Yip.*" Consuela had no problem with that. All things considered, she preferred living on the beach.

The landline next to my bed rang. I reached for the receiver. "Hello."

"*Bonjour, Mademoiselle Fields. Ghislain Lambert est au téléphone. Est-ce que vous voulez lui parler?*"

I really didn't want to talk to anyone. Least of all Ghislain Lambert. "*Oui. Merci.*"

"*Je vais transférer l'appel.*"

The phone clicked and Ghislain said, "Allo."

"Hello."

"I'm so glad I finally reached you. I've been worried. How are you?"

"I'm fine."

"I should have asked you to spend the night."

As if I'd ever have spent the night with a man I didn't know. "Really. I'm fine."

"May I take you to lunch?"

"Today?"

"Yes. Today. I need to see with my own eyes that you are well."

"I'm not leaving the Ritz."

"I'll take you to Bar Vendôme."

In a perfect world, I'd spend my day curled up on a couch with Consuela, ordering room service, and arguing with Thor about Mr. Brown's ridiculous plan. "Um…"

"You have to eat."

"It's very nice of you, but—"

"Please?"

Ghislain Lambert was the reason I was in Paris. If Mr. Brown was right, if he was cleaning money for drug dealers, Ghislain deserved to be in jail. "What time?"

"One o'clock?"

"I'll see you there." I hung up the phone. Lunch at Bar Vendôme would be safe. There was no way Javier Diaz's people would make an attempt on my life inside the Ritz.

Working with that belief, I snuck in a massage at the Chanel spa. The masseuse who worked on my neck and shoulders told me my muscles were tight.

As understatements went, it was enormous.

At one o'clock, I walked into the cherry-wood-paneled Bar Vendôme. The restaurant was full. A table of Chinese tourists chatted in Mandarin (it could have been Cantonese—I didn't know enough to tell the difference). A gaunt model picked at a salad and listened to a man in a business suit. An American family—two bored teenagers and a set of parents—perused menus. Perused until the kids spotted me. Then their phones came out.

I pretended not to notice they were snapping pictures.

The teenagers were girls, so maybe they were taking pictures of Thor. He stood behind me in all his better-looking-than-Chris-Hemsworth glory.

Ghislain was already seated at a table for two. He had the French knack for looking *comme il faut*—more than stylish, effortlessly stylish. He wore a navy-blue blazer, a blue and white striped shirt (probably from Charvet), and an Hermès tie. He was reading something on his cell and looking down his nose to do it.

He raised his head, spotted me in the doorway, and put his phone on the table. A charming smile split his face and he stood.

He was a bad man. He cleaned money for drug dealers.

"I don't want to do this," I whispered without moving my lips.

Thor grunted. "Can't say as I blame you."

I forced my feet forward and endured Ghislain's kisses next to my cheeks.

Thor found himself a seat at the bar.

"*Ça va?*" Ghislain asked as we sat in comfortable chairs covered in paprika velvet.

"Fine, thanks. And you?"

He waved away my question. "What happened last night?" Ghislain caught a waiter's eye and nodded almost imperceptibly.

The waiter came immediately. "*Oui, monsieur?*"

Ghislain smiled at me. "Wine?"

"No. Thank you. An Aperol spritz."

"You don't mind?" Ghislain held up the wine list.

"Of course not."

He ordered a glass of Domaine Lucien Crochet Sancerre.

The waiter disappeared and Ghislain leaned forward. "Now, tell me. What happened?"

"A car followed us. Shots were fired."

He pursed his lips as if my explanation wasn't good enough. "I saw the pictures. The back end of that car was completely destroyed."

I shrugged. "We were lucky. Viktor's father's car saved us."

"But why was someone shooting at you?"

Ghislain might be laundering Javier's money. Ghislain might be in Javier's pocket. I managed a small smile. "It's possible someone in the Sinaloa Cartel wants me dead."

"But wh—"

"Ghislain." A woman in a gray skirt and simple white cotton blouse stood next to our table. She'd tied a cashmere sweater around her neck with casual elegance. Her shoes were Chanel flats. The handbag hanging from the crook of her arm was a Kelly. Her face was a study in sharp planes, strong brows, and deep-set brown eyes—a sweep of bangs across the high forehead softened her enough to be approachable.

Ghislain stood. "*Marie-Claude, ça va?*"

They spoke in rapid French. Marie-Claude was just back from her house in the country. She'd arrived in Paris to discover (*quelle horreur*) a leak in her apartment. She was staying at the Ritz while a plumber repaired the pipes.

The phone Ghislain had left on the table buzzed and a message appeared on its screen.

A left-handed child, I'd been writing upside down my whole life. And reading upside down. Reading Ghislain's text was easy.

Les transferts n'ont pas été envoyés. Y-a-t-il un problème?

What transfers? Why hadn't they been sent? What was the problem? I committed the sender's number to memory and looked up at Ghislain and Marie-Claude before he could catch me snooping. Just in time, too. Ghislain remembered he'd invited me to lunch. "Marie-Claude, allow me to introduce you to Poppy Fields. Poppy, my cousin, Marie-Claude de Savary."

I saw dismissal in her eyes the instant Ghislain uttered my name. I was *une Américaine*. Without uttering a word she said I was naïve, conventional, materialistic, uncultured, rude, and gun-loving. One or two of those things might have been true.

"*Un plaisir,*" she murmured with a stiff smile.

"Likewise."

We were both lying.

Ghislain's eagerness to know me was atypical. Most French people, especially Parisians, reacted to Americans as Marie-Claude had—with a barely hidden sneer and deep-rooted sense of superiority.

"Won't you join us?" I smiled sweetly.

"Sadly, I must meet with a plumber."

"What a pity."

"Ghislain—" she turned to her cousin "—*à bientôt*."

"Au revoir." Ghislain resumed his seat and glanced at his phone. The color drained from his face and he snatched the device off the table.

"A problem?" I asked.

"A small one." He put the phone facedown and offered me a sickly smile. "It's nothing."

And people said I was a bad liar.

The waiter returned with our drinks.

Ghislain's wine had barely touched the table before he had the glass wrapped tightly in his hand and the rim at his lips.

"Your cousin is charming."

Ghislain blinked. Did I not realize I'd been snubbed in favor of a plumber?

Mr. Brown had told me to convince Ghislain I wasn't very smart. Mission accomplished.

"Our grandfathers were brothers. We've always been close."

"I see." I sipped my Aperol and smiled. "Tell me about your work."

An hour later, I knew about every famous client Ghislain had.

And I'd thought bankers were supposed to be discreet.

There was a French popstar with a sex addiction. An Italian skier who blew through money faster than his time in the Super-G. The son of a sheik who carefully hid his penchant for being dominated by women with whips. I learned more than I'd ever wanted to know about the über-rich's private penchants, but nothing about laundering drug money.

I finished my salad and wiped my lips with a linen napkin. "I hope I'm not keeping you from something important."

Ghislain looked up from the remains of his lobster. "Not at all."

"I worried those texts might be important." His cell had buzzed throughout our lunch.

The sickly smile returned. "No, no." He scanned the surrounding tables as if he might find a new topic sitting at one. "How long are you in Paris?"

"I don't know. It's up to my mother." She was the excuse for my extended stay.

"What was it like growing up with a movie-star mother?"

I'd been asked that exact question a million times.

The usual answer slipped effortlessly past my lips. "At home she was just my mother."

He nodded as if I'd said something deep, rested his arms on the table, and leaned closer to me. "I'd like to take you out to dinner."

"Someone is trying to kill me."

He waved away my objection. "We'll have dinner at my apartment. It's a secure building. You'd be safe there."

And maybe I'd be able to snoop. "Just the two of us?" My voice was breathy. Who knew I could channel Marilyn Monroe? "I'd like that."

Ghislain's pupils grew large. "I'll call you."

"You'll need my cell number." I rattled off the digits.

He fumbled with his cell. "Too fast!"

"Let me." I held out my hand for his phone.

Our fingers touched. His skin was ice cold. So cold I almost flinched.

I took the phone and called my cell. "Now I have your

number, too." And maybe John Brown could get a subpoena to hack it. I snuck a glance at Thor, who was scanning the room for threats. He was completely unaware every woman in the bar was staring at him.

Ghislain's phone, still in my hand, buzzed, reclaiming my attention. I glanced at the screen and read, Où es-tu? Votre situation est ténue. *Where are you? Your situation is tenuous.* It was the same sender as earlier. I handed the phone back to Ghislain. "I am keeping you from something important."

He looked at the screen and paled. "It is not important."

If that were true, he wouldn't look as if he was about to lose his lobster.

He waved his hand in an elegant dismissal. "It's the work of a moment. Just a few transfers and my client will be happy again."

"Still, your client seems distressed. I shouldn't keep you." I pushed my chair away from the table.

Ghislain pulled two two-hundred-euro notes from his wallet and tossed them next to his plate. He stood. "I'll call you about dinner. Soon."

"I'd like that." Had I said one true thing throughout the whole lunch? I stood and smoothed my pants over my hips.

Something dark flickered in his eyes and his tongue darted past his lips. "I will call soon."

Thor pushed away from the bar and watched Ghislain kiss the air next to my cheeks.

Together we watched Ghislain scurry down the hallway, head down, phone in hand. Only his back was visible, but I was willing to bet he was texting like a madman. Certainly something had grabbed his attention, because he was completely oblivious to the small mountain of Louis Vuitton luggage stacked in front of him.

He walked right into it.

Tumbled right over it.

The phone in his hand flew.

My knowledge of French curse words was encyclopedic, but I'd never heard them strung together the way Ghislain used them.

Ghislain extricated himself from the pile of suitcases and muttered something to the Asian woman standing next to the tipped bags.

Whatever he said couldn't have been polite—an expression of absolute shock crossed the woman's face.

Ghislain scooped up his phone and scurried off.

"He's a real gentleman," observed Thor.

"A dying breed."

"Did you learn anything?"

"I'm not sure. Maybe." I closed my eyes and made sure the number I'd memorized was still stored in my brain. It was. "Ghislain Lambert is totally terrified. I'm just not sure of whom."

TEN

Yurgi Prokorhov had booked the chef's table at La Maison. Unlike the rest of the restaurant (which looked as if the designer had filched the furniture from Versailles), the chef's table was simple. No gilt. No brocade. No fat-cheeked cherubs. Glass walls offered guests lucky enough to be seated at the table a three-hundred-and-sixty-degree view of a working kitchen.

What was happening in the kitchen was an elaborate dance in a stainless-steel ballroom. A sous-chef watched over a boucher, a poissonnier, a friturier, a grillardin, a pâtissier, a saucier, and a légumier. And those were just the cooks I could see.

One of Yurgi's guards stood just outside the kitchen doors. Thor stood just outside the door to our glass box.

Unless one of the chefs moonlighted as an assassin, we were safe.

"That's Alain Rivard." Chariss nodded her chin toward a man in a white chef's coat and hat. Awe made her breathless.

"He is cooking for us tonight," said Yurgi. "A special menu."

In a country where top chefs were more famous than rock

stars, Alain Rivard stood alone. Having him cook just for us was akin to having Adele perform a private concert.

Chariss smiled bravely. She might recognize Alain Rivard, but that didn't mean she wanted to eat his food. Chariss was not an adventurous eater. Her usual dinner was a green salad with a squeeze of lemon juice and grilled salmon or chicken on top. Plus, she had to fit into her costumes in the morning.

The black-clad waiter put *amuse bouche* in front of us. He explained the tiny bit of food art was actually a poached quail egg on an English pea *velouté*.

Gamely, I picked up my fork.

With a tenuous smile, Chariss did the same.

Of course, the little egg was sublime.

Viktor, who was looking dazed by his proximity to Chariss, wolfed his in one bite. "Please, tell me about your film."

"This one is all action," Chariss replied. "It's about a woman who accidentally gets involved with a drug cartel, then disrupts their operation."

"Art imitating life?" asked Yurgi.

"Movies aren't real. What Poppy did may yet get her killed." Chariss actually sounded worried. She shot me a mother-hen look that communicated her opinion of my plan to go out later in the evening.

My opinion of the plan wasn't much different. I narrowed my eyes and stared at Thor's unresponsive back. Thus far, he hadn't shared much of John Brown's scheme with me. Both of them were treating me as if I was a ditzy girl who couldn't handle the truth.

I relaxed my jaw and returned my attention to the people at the table. Chariss and Viktor were talking movies.

Yurgi patted my hand. "My son loves cinema. He wants to produce films."

Chariss had a pet project or two and Viktor had the money

to make them happen. It was a match made in heaven. "I'm sure she has lots of helpful advice."

"Then we will let them talk. Tell me—" Yurgi took a sip of his wine "—why does this drug lord want you dead?"

Yurgi looked absolutely nothing like my father, but something about him reminded me of my dad. An almost overwhelming urge to tell him everything took hold of me. I twisted the napkin in my lap.

"I'll keep your secret. I promise."

I looked into Yurgi's dark eyes and believed him. "The night I escaped I saw—"

The door to our glass box swung open and Alain Rivard sailed inside. "*Bon soir.*" He told us what we would be eating. He gave us the ingredients' provenance. Kissing his fingertips, he explained how each course would be perfectly prepared, then asked us if we had any questions.

I waited for Chariss to request a salad.

Wisely, she kept her mouth shut.

Having reminded us who the real star was in his kitchen and having sufficiently piqued our appetites, Chef Rivard returned to his stove.

Chariss immediately returned her attention to Viktor. "That idea I was telling you about…" I'd been right. She was pitching pet projects.

"Your mother is a smart businesswoman," observed Yurgi.

I didn't argue.

"What do you do?"

I was an under-trained spy. But I couldn't tell him that. "I wrote a book. My agent is finalizing the contract."

"You wrote a book? A novel?"

"Yes."

"You are an artist like your mother."

"I can't act."

His eyes twinkled. "I prefer books."

"What sorts of businesses do you run?"

"Real estate. Banks. A bit of oil."

"May I ask you a banking question?"

"Of course."

"It's about money launder—" My voice faltered at the suddenly dark expression in his eyes. I gathered my courage and continued, "After my experience in Mexico—" I checked his eyes—the darkness had lightened "—I wondered how it all works."

"How so?"

"In the United States drug money is in small bills. I read somewhere that a kilo of cocaine weighs three kilos in currency."

Yurgi nodded.

"Smurfs deposit cash—"

"Smurfs?"

"That's what they're called in the US. They're people who deposit illegal money into bank accounts. The deposit is always less than the ten thousand dollar reporting threshold."

"I understand now."

I took a sip of wine. "What I don't get is the scale. Google says drug revenues in the United States top one hundred billion dollars a year. That's at least ten million deposits to sneak past regulators."

"My banks do everything possible to comply with international standards." The darkness in Yurgi's eyes had returned and his voice was colder than Siberia in January.

Perfect. There was already a hitman after me and now I'd angered an oligarch with unlimited resources. "I didn't mean to imply you're involved."

His expression softened to Siberia in March. He stared at me for a moment, considering my intentions. "Think about places where people spend cash. Casinos. Amusement parks. Resorts. Race tracks." He shifted his gaze to the busy kitchen. "Successful restaurants and clubs. In places like this, dirty money mixes with clean."

I nodded. And waited for more.

"After the money makes it into a bank, the shell game begins."

"The shell game?"

"Shell corporations transfer the money from account to account until it is used to buy a racehorse or a Gulfstream or —" his gaze returned to the kitchen "—an exquisite meal with beautiful women."

"What are you two whispering about?" asked Chariss.

"Racehorses," replied Yurgi.

"Poppy loves horses. Always has."

Yurgi raised one of his bushy brows.

"It's true. I grew up in Montana. Dad put me on a horse before I could walk."

Viktor tore his gaze away from Chariss. "My father has a horse being groomed for the Prix de l'Arc."

That was impressive. The Prix de l'Arc was one of the most storied races in Europe. "I hear the new track is amazing."

"I will take you to see it," Yurgi promised.

A waiter served our next course.

Chariss made charming Yurgi her mission. She asked him about his racehorse, made him laugh till tears stood in his eyes with the story of the disastrous time she rode a horse for a role, then entertained us all with anecdotes about actors and actresses most people wished they knew.

Shortly after perfect citron tartes were served, Chariss shifted in her chair. "This has been such a lovely evening. I hate for it to end, but I have an early call in the morning."

Yurgi, entirely charmed, smiled at her. "A night to remember. Thank you for joining us."

We returned to the hotel without a single shot fired.

Yurgi and Viktor walked us to our suite. Thor trailed behind.

Yurgi bent over my hand, barely brushing his lips across

my skin. "This danger you are in, it will not last. When it is over, I will take you to ParisLongchamp. It is a promise."

"I'd like that."

When Chariss and I closed the door on our Russian friends, she asked, "Are you still going out?"

I glanced at Thor.

He nodded.

I nodded.

Chariss crossed her arms. "I'm tired. I'm taking a sleeping pill. Try not to get yourself killed." Apparently, she was still mad at me.

"I'll do my best."

Without another word, she disappeared into her bedroom.

I let Consuela out of my bedroom, then turned to Thor. "What's the plan?"

"Change clothes."

"What's wrong with what I'm wearing?" The little black dress and heels were classics.

"You can't run in that." The man had a point.

"Fine. Would you please walk Consuela while I change?"

He hesitated.

"Nothing is going to happen in this suite."

He nodded and clipped Consuela's leash to her collar.

I went to my room and changed into the outfit I'd bought earlier—without sunglasses, scarf, or pink trench. My nerves jittered as I touched up my lipstick.

My nerves jittered worse when I walked into the bar, Le Squelette, in the Latin Quarter. With its exposed stone walls, the interior felt like a cave—a cave of no return. Someone had painted the ceiling with blackboard paint and an artist, one who would never see his work in a reputable gallery, had rendered a variety of skeletons in chalk.

The actual bar, nicked and dinged and creaky, was painted black. Flickering LED lights illuminated bottles of questionable liquor. The whole place reeked of cigarettes.

It was the kind of bar frequented by locals—and only locals. No self-respecting tourist, not even the most assiduous searcher of local color, would come in here.

Three men gaped at me. Three men and the blousy woman with her hand on the beer tap.

"What do you want?" The woman wiped a grayed rag across the top of the bar. "Kronenbourg 1664." A bottle of beer seemed the safest choice. Testing my luck with the cleanliness of the glassware or the contents of the liquor bottles seemed totally reckless.

The woman didn't move, and it occurred to me she hadn't been asking for my drink order. She wanted to know why I was in her bar.

"Just the beer. In a bottle." I pulled a ten-euro note out of my handbag.

She took the money, opened the beer, and put the bottle on the bar next to a cloudy glass. She did not offer me change.

I took the bottle, left the glass, and chose a table where my back could press against the stone wall.

Outside, Thor and John Brown's men were watching me. They wouldn't let anything happen. At least I hoped not. I crossed my fingers in my lap, took a tiny sip of beer, and looked at the three men holding up the bar. With nicotine-stained teeth, grubby scarves wrapped round their scrawny necks, and listless expressions, they looked as if they belonged there.

This was the place John Brown had set his trap?

Were the full-of-local-color bartender and patrons actually his agents?

I relaxed. Slightly.

I took another sip of beer and waited for something to happen.

It didn't. Not after ten minutes. Not after twenty. I picked the Kronenbourg label off the bottle. Not after forty-five. I ordered a second beer just so I could have something on the table. Not after an hour. I called Thor and asked, "How long am I supposed to stay here?"

"Five more minutes."

"Fine, but just so you know, I would never wait this long for a real person."

"I don't doubt you for a second, princess." He hung up before I could come up with a smart reply.

I ground my teeth, waited another five pointless minutes, and walked outside.

A soft, clinging mist filled the streets, giving the light posts halos and making Le Squelette's dim lights appear far more inviting than they actually were. The mist was cold, and I hadn't brought an umbrella. I turned up the collar of my trench coat and set off down the hill.

Mr. Brown had picked a bar on a street that didn't allow cars. If I wanted a cab (I desperately wanted a cab), I'd have to walk a few blocks.

My loafers' heels rang against the cobblestones. Rainwater trickled down my neck.

If someone was following me, I'd know. I'd hear them. And Thor was out there somewhere—watching.

I stopped and glanced over my shoulder.

Did that shadow move? Was it one of the good guys?

My heart fluttered in my chest and I jammed my shaking hands in my pocket. I was being silly. There were people— good people—watching. Just because I couldn't see them didn't mean they weren't there.

I passed shuttered butcher shops and bakeries and a tabac with dirty windows and a flashing sign for *cigarettes electroniques.*

Up ahead, there were lights and traffic and people.

I would not glance over my shoulder again—I would not.

I stepped onto the sidewalk of an actual street and realized my hopes for traffic and people had been optimistic.

Except for a taxi lumbering toward me, the street was deserted. I waved.

Thor and John Brown and whoever else was behind me could figure out what had gone wrong at Le Squelette on their own. I was going back to the Ritz.

The phone in my pocket buzzed.

I held it to my ear as I walked toward the cab. "Yes?"

"What are you doing?"

"Going back to the hotel. It's late. I'm tired. No one is coming."

"Don't—"

I hung up and opened the taxi's back door. "The Ritz au Place Vendôme?"

"*Oui.*"

I climbed into the taxi, rested my head against the backseat, and closed my eyes. What were the chances that the paparazzi had moved on? I'd seen on the news that Beyoncé was in Paris. Maybe the photographers had given up on me for a woman who'd actually earned her fame. A woman could dream.

I opened my eyes and caught a glimpse of Tour Montparnasse. "You're going the wrong way."

The driver didn't respond.

I tried again. This time in French. "*Vous conduisez dans la mauvaise direction.*"

The driver looked over his shoulder. His grin told me I was an idiot woman who'd climbed into the wrong cab. What was next? A gun to my head?

Using my trench to hide my hand, my fingers tightened on the door handle. The next time we came to a stop, I'd run.

The light ahead turned yellow.

I was ready. Blood pumped through my legs. My focus narrowed. My mouth dried.

The taxi slowed. Stopped.

I yanked on the door handle and nothing happened.

Nothing. I fumbled for a lock. Dammit. The light was going to turn green. Giving up on stealth, I felt for a lock with both hands.

There wasn't one.

"*Vous ne pouvez pas échapper.*" You can't escape.

We'd just see about that. I slid over to the other side of the car and searched for a lock.

Nothing.

"Where are you taking me?" My French had left me.

"*Quelqu'un veut vouz parler.*" Someone wants to talk to you.

"Who? Who wants to talk to me?" And why?

The driver didn't respond.

"Where are you taking me?"

Still no response.

I had my cell. Surely Thor and Mr. Brown were tracking my cell. Or—duh—I could call them. I pulled the phone out of my pocket.

The driver jerked the wheel and pulled the car to the curb behind a black sedan.

Two men climbed out of the car and ran toward us. One of them opened my door and grabbed the phone out of my hand. He crushed it beneath the heel of his shoe.

I looked up at him and the cab didn't seem so bad. I wrapped the seatbelt around my wrist and held on.

He reached into the backseat, grabbed my free arm, and pulled.

I held onto that seatbelt. No way was I letting go.

He pulled harder.

I kicked, connecting with something that made the man grunt in pain. I might have lasted until help arrived if it weren't for the second man. I was kicking at the first one when a sharp pinch of pain in my arm made me turn—just in time to see the second man inject me with something.

I came to in the back of a new car. Someone had stuffed

my mouth with cotton—at least it felt like it. I ran my tongue over my teeth and listened.

Two men in the front seat were speaking in Arabic.

Arabic? What was going on?

Slowly I reached for my pocket, then remembered (with sickening clarity) my phone was in pieces on a Parisian sidewalk. Thor had no way to find me.

This made no sense. Why was I being kidnapped? The taxi driver could have shot me. The man who'd injected my arm could have filled me with poison. Why was I still alive?

Unless…unless someone wanted me dead and someone else wanted me kidnapped.

I knew who wanted me dead. "Where are you taking me? Who wants to talk to me?"

The front passenger—the man who'd sunk a needle into my arm—turned. *"Á Ahmed Badawi. Il a des questions pour vous."* To Ahmed Badawi. He has questions for you.

They were taking me to a terrorist. I pushed myself to sitting. "He could have just called."

ELEVEN

I was lost. Absolutely lost. I didn't recognize a single land-mark—no Notre Dame, no Louvre, not even Sacré-Couer. We drove through a Paris I didn't know.

This Paris wasn't pretty. The buildings were modern. And ugly. And marked with graffiti. Trash littered the sidewalks—sodden newspapers, cigarette butts, crumpled fast food packaging.

The streets were near empty. The few people I did see were men. Were we in a no-go zone? A district where women weren't welcome?

The temperature in the car was too warm, but I shivered.

The men in the front of the car ignored me. I figured that was a good thing.

We pulled into a parking lot behind a dark loading dock. The car's headlights illuminated graffiti and metal garage doors. A startled animal skittered across the cracked concrete. The man in the passenger seat got out of the car and jabbed at a keypad.

I shivered harder.

Slowly the metal door rolled up, revealing a storage space.

The man returned to the car, opened my door, and jerked his head toward the gaping entryway.

My mouth was dry. My head was fuzzy. My feet were heavy. Exiting the car was a logistical challenge. Foot there. Arm here. Slide.

"*Dépêche toi.*"

I resisted scowling at him. Barely. It was amazing how awful I felt. My stomach was queasy. My head ached. My muscles felt foreign. There wasn't any "hurry up" in me.

I slid closer to the door. But not fast enough.

He reached inside the car and jerked me into the night air. Then he pushed me forward.

I tripped over my heavy feet and landed on my hands and knees. A piece of broken glass sliced my palm and pain cut through the fog in my brain. I stayed on the ground for a moment, breathing air tinged with smog and urine.

Behind me, one of the men laughed, a nasty sound that exactly suited our surroundings.

A hand squeezed my upper arm and yanked me to standing.

This time when the man pushed, I didn't fall.

I stumbled forward, into the dark maw of the storage space.

The door rumbled shut behind me and the lights came on. Single bulbs hanging from frayed cords buzzed as if the electricity powering them was suspect.

I swallowed and took stock.

Two men with hard faces held me captive. I was in a part of Paris as foreign to me as the moon. And there was the bone-chilling possibility that one of the most dangerous men on the planet was coming here to talk to me.

On the plus side, the two men who'd driven me here thought I was weak.

I wasn't. And with each passing second, I felt more like myself.

Another swallow. Badawi wasn't here. Not yet. Now might be my best chance to run. What could I use to escape?

Wooden crates were stacked against one wall. Army cots lined a second wall. A scarred table on the third wall served as a desk for a laptop, various tools, and a tangle of stray wires.

One of the men shoved me forward. Again.

I fell. Again. My hands connected with the gritty concrete floor and pain shot through my wrists.

A rusty discolored stain next to me caught my attention. Blood?

Things really couldn't get any worse.

Then the door lifted.

Another three men entered the garage. I recognized one. Ahmed Badawi's face was easily recognizable. A jagged scar ran from the corner of his left eye to the base of his ear. I'd looked him up on the FBI's Most Wanted website after I watched his nephew die in a dining room in Mexico. According to the FBI, Badawi had a doctorate in economics, and was a drug lord, an arms dealer, and a terrorist.

I'd also googled him. Google said the house he'd lived in as a child had been bombed with him in it. He was the lone survivor of the blast. With his parents dead, he went to live with his married sister and her husband, a man who taught him how to kill those who'd killed his loved ones.

Badawi looked at me with expressionless eyes. "You were there when my nephew died?" He spoke English with an accent that said he'd learned the language at Eton.

My mouth was too dry to speak. I held my hand to my throat and nodded.

"What happened?" he insisted.

"May I have some water?" I croaked. "Please?"

Badawi barked something in Arabic and one of the men opened a cooler next to the desk and pulled out a bottle of water.

He thrust the bottle into my hands and I drank. Each sip added a tiny bit to my reserves. There had to be a way out of here.

"Tell me." Badawi's brows drew together and his beard did nothing to hide his frown. He was done waiting on me.

"We were eating dinner at Ignacio Quintero's hacienda when the Zetas attacked. They launched a grenade into the house. Your nephew was killed instantly."

Badawi's nephew had been there to negotiate the importation of heroine but he'd struck me as a spoiled boy playing at being a man.

"He was the only one who died?"

"Lots of people died that night." I'd even killed a few of them.

"Who else was there when my nephew died?"

"Just me. Diaz wasn't there. He left a minute before the Zetas started shooting. Quintero realized we were under attack and ran away."

"And you?" There was an unmistakable sneer in Badawi's voice. How had I, a mere woman, survived while his nephew perished? "What happened to you?"

"The table fell on me. If it hadn't, I'd be dead, too."

Badawi stroked his beard. "Quintero ran?"

"Yes."

"How did he die?"

Images from that awful night filled my head. The throat-clogging smell of blood. The shrieks of men dying. The desperate escape from the hacienda. I'd been terrified that night. I was terrified now. I wiped my palms (one bloody, the other sweaty) against my trench. "He was shot."

"You saw this? You're sure he's dead?"

I nodded. "I'm positive."

"And what of Diaz?"

I glanced around at Badawi's lair—nothing about the concrete space said he planned on dropping me at the Ritz when we'd finished talking. The rusty stain on the floor suggested the opposite. This might well be the last conversation I ever had. If it was, I wanted Diaz to pay for all the horrible things he'd done. I lifted my chin. "Diaz survived because he was working with the Zetas. He betrayed Quintero. He's responsible for your nephew's death."

A sadistic smile spread across Badawi's narrow face. A razor thin, ruthless smile. The smile of a man who'd had his suspicions confirmed. The smile of a man who would enjoy killing Diaz.

I drank the last sip of water in the bottle.

"How do you know?"

"I was there. I heard him say so." Hands down, that night was the worst night of my life. Up till tonight.

Badawi nodded and said something in Arabic to one of the men who'd come in with him.

The man punched at a button and the metal door rose.

That was it? We were done?

The most-wanted terrorist in the world turned his back on me.

"Wait." I wished the word back as soon as it left my lips.

Badawi glanced at me over his shoulder.

"What happens now?"

He shrugged. "No one can know I'm in France." He spoke to the two men who'd brought me here. Whatever he said made them smile. Coarse, lascivious smiles.

"I won't tell anyone." It was a desperate plea.

"No," he agreed. "You won't."

Badawi and his two guards left without another word. When the door closed behind them, the men who'd brought me to this place circled. They were predators who liked to play with their prey before the kill.

I glanced again at the rusty stain on the floor and shuddered.

The man who'd been the passenger in the car said something and the driver laughed.

Dread trickled down my spine.

They took their time. Circling. Laughing. Savoring what they thought was my fear.

"*Mon frère est mort,*" said the passenger.

His brother was dead? What did that have to do with me? Unless...unless he was one of the men who'd died at Antoine's.

"*Tu vas souffrir.*"

If he was as big as Thor or Viktor, I'd be more worried. The man who threatened me hardly outweighed me.

The more the two men circled, the more they laughed, the more pissed off I became. What if I was just some poor unfortunate girl with no way to defend herself?

I inched closer to the desk.

When the driver grabbed me, I was only a few feet from my goal.

His arm circled my throat and he pulled my back against his chest.

I dropped my weight and rolled my shoulder into his chest, freeing myself from his grasp. The look of shock on his face was almost comical.

I scanned the table. The pen on the corner would do.

But now, the passenger, the man who'd pushed me down twice, the man who wanted me to suffer for his brother's death, was coming at me.

I kicked, and my foot connected with his groin. He grunted and doubled over. While he was bent, I chopped the back of his neck with my forearms. He fell to the floor with a satisfying *oomph*.

He was down, but he wasn't out. When he recovered, he'd be like an enraged bull. I had to be ready.

The driver said something in Arabic. The words were a

mystery, but their meaning was clear. They were going to hurt me. Slowly. I would wish for death.

I raced the last few feet to the desk and my fingers scrabbled for the pen on the corner. Got it. I clutched it in my fingers.

The driver looked at the pen in my hand and snickered.

He didn't believe I could cause him harm. With the carelessness of a man who's sure he'll prevail, he rushed toward me, telegraphing his intentions with every shift of his shoulders.

I stepped out of his way.

Almost.

Somehow, he caught my hair. And he was pulling. And it hurt like hell.

"Let go."

He used my hair to yank me closer to him.

Which was fine. I had to be close enough to damage him.

It was almost as if he was pulling my knee to his groin. I added some force of my own.

He grunted and his eyes teared up, but he held onto my hair.

I kneed him a second time.

The passenger was moving. Groaning. Muttering something about all the horrible things he'd do to me just as soon as he stood.

I was almost out of time.

My knee met the driver's junk a third time. He loosened his hold on my hair and he fell to the floor.

I spun and faced the passenger. His face was distorted with rage and his fingers had curled into talons.

I tightened my grip on the pen.

The passenger charged towards me, his hands ready to choke the life out of me.

He never expected me to charge back. Nor did he expect

me to stab him in the neck with a ballpoint pen. He staggered backward, his hands at his own throat.

Now the driver was moving. He'd already pushed himself up to his hands and knees.

I retreated to the desk and grabbed the laptop. Holding it with both hands, I brought the casing down on the driver's head. Twice. Maybe three times. Okay, four (I was scared and angry and I didn't want him waking up). Then I turned back to the passenger.

He stared at me with hate-filled eyes. His mouth moved, but no words came out. Blood welled between his fingers. So much blood.

That much blood, I had to have punctured his carotid artery.

The passenger was going into shock. The passenger was going to die.

And it didn't bother me. Not one bit. What would Thor say about the state of my soul?

I dropped the laptop on the floor, skirted the dying man, and raced to the door.

Unlike a garage door opener, there was no single button. I needed the code. Without it, I was trapped.

I tried 1-2-3-4.

The door didn't budge.

I looked back toward my captors. One was beyond giving me a code, the second probably was.

If I couldn't punch in the right numbers, maybe I could disable the system and raise the door manually. A good idea, if I had any idea how to do that.

Dammit. I had to get out of here. Fast.

At some point, someone was going to come back—if only to help dispose of my body.

I glanced at the wooden crates. Maybe they held something I could use to jack the door high enough for me to wriggle out.

With legs made heavy by draining adrenaline, I hurried over to the crates. Several were empty and of no help. I opened one with a lid and peered inside.

Oh, hell.

The terrorists would definitely be back. The crate was filled with guns.

A second crate held ball bearings.

Why would anyone need that many tiny balls? Unless…

I glanced back toward the desk and the tangle of wires. Someone had been building bombs.

I had to get out of here. I needed to warn someone. Right away. I'd tell them that Badawi was planning an attack, that there might be suicide bombers, that I had not one specific detail.

Breaking that laptop over the driver's head had been a mistake.

I braced my hands on the edge of the crate and lowered my head. How did I get myself into these messes?

One thing was certain, I couldn't leave here without that laptop.

I straightened and forced myself back to the desk.

I couldn't look at the passenger. Could not. Maybe I wasn't as immune to feelings about his death as I thought.

I scooped up the laptop (ignoring the blood on its casing) and lugged it back to the door. The keypad mocked me.

I could do this. I had to. If I were a terrorist, what numbers would I pick? I propped the computer against the wall and tried 0-9-1-1. Nothing happened. I tried 0-9-1-1-0-1. The door didn't move.

I sank my head into my hands.

We were in France.

With a shaking finger, I entered 1-1-1-3-1-5.

The door lifted. Slowly. I'd done it! Now all I had to do was get out of the most dangerous neighborhood in Paris in one piece.

I bent for the computer and saw feet on the other side of the door.

My heart rose to my throat. They were back already?

Why hadn't I stolen one of the guns out of the crate?

Without bullets it had seemed sort of pointless.

I drew the laptop back as if it were a Louisville Slugger.

The door was more than halfway up, revealing legs, a hand, and a Glock on the other side.

I tightened my grip on the laptop. My shoulder muscles bunched. I had seconds.

The door lifted all the way.

I swung, my arms doing what they'd planned even as my brain registered the man in front of me.

Jake ducked. "Easy does it."

"What the hell are you doing here?" I'd never been so happy to see anyone in my life.

His golden smile cut through the darkness. "I thought you might need some help."

"How did you find me?"

He lifted his shoulders in a so-sue-me shrug and pointed at my locket.

He'd done this once before—put a tracking device in the necklace I always wore—so I shouldn't be surprised. I couldn't be angry.

I stepped past him into the night. Mist hung heavy in the air and carried the scent of metal and rotting food and despair.

Jake looked past me and spotted the bodies. His lips thinned. "What happened?"

Now I shrugged. "They had plans for me. Do you have a car?"

"What's going on?"

"Badawi was here. He's planning something—something terrible."

"Ahmed Badawi?"

I nodded, suddenly too tired for words.

"He was here?" Jake sounded incredulous.

"That's what I just said." My legs shook with the effort of standing.

Jake didn't seem to notice. "He's supposed to be in a cave in Pakistan."

"Tell him that."

"We need to get out of here."

Well, duh.

TWELVE

I settled into the passenger's seat of Jake's car and stowed the battered laptop at my feet.

"I'll be back in a minute." Jake locked the car doors and left me there. He disappeared inside the building.

I sat, my eyelids at half-mast, almost too tired to move.

A nearby train roared through the night and the air vibrated with the violence of its passing. I closed my eyes all the way and thought about the crate of ball bearings, wires tangled across the scarred desk, and the misery they promised.

Tap, tap.

I jumped.

Jake stood by the window. "What's the code?"

"The code?"

"To close the door."

"Eleven, thirteen, fifteen."

He stared at me for a long second, then turned on his heel, returned to the metal door, and punched in the numbers.

A moment later, Jake climbed into the car and wrapped his fingers around the wheel.

I waited for him to start the engine, but he didn't move.

"You killed a man with a pen." He didn't look at me. Instead he stared out into the darkness.

"It was him or me."

"What did you do to the other guy?"

"He's dead, too?" My stomach sank.

"Yeah."

The laptop at my feet drew my gaze.

Jake's gaze followed mine. "You're kidding. You beat him to death with a computer?"

"I hit him on the head." Four times. "Can we go now? Please?"

Jake started the car and looked at me out of the corner of his eye. "I have to make a call."

"Whatever." I was too tired to care what he did as long as he got me as far away as possible from the men I'd killed.

With the phone pressed between his ear and his shoulder, Jake put the car in reverse. "We have a problem." He glanced my way and a grimace darkened his features. "She's with me. She's fine." That was debatable. "She says she saw Ahmed Badawi and—"

Jake listened.

"Yes, sir. Ahmed Badawi. She killed two of Badawi's men and the place where they were keeping her—"

He shifted to drive and merged into traffic. "Yes, sir. She killed them."

A driver in a beat-up Renault honked at us.

Jake swerved. "I'm sure they're dead, sir." He glanced my way a second time. "I'm bringing her in."

I closed my eyes.

"The place where they were holding her—" Jake's voice seemed to come from a great distance "—we need a team there as soon as possible."

The seats of Jake's car felt like heaven—soft leather, lumbar support, heated—so much like heaven I couldn't worry about whatever was coming next.

"They were making suicide vests."

I'd heard enough. More death was more than I could handle. I leaned my head against the window and let my exhausted body drift to sleep.

"Poppy, wake up. We're here."

"Stop poking me." I opened my eyes. Jake had parked in an enclosed courtyard. "Where are we?"

"Neuilly sur Seine."

I was so not in the mood for the suburbs. "What are we doing here?"

"Someone's cranky."

"I'm entitled." I was *so* entitled. "Why aren't we at the Ritz?"

"We're at a safe house." That didn't exactly answer my question.

"Why?" I insisted.

"Mr. Brown wants to talk to you." Jake used a tone most people saved for recalcitrant toddlers.

"Oh, joy."

Jake made a sound that might—might—have been a laugh.

"I mean it. Take me to my hotel. Please. All I want is a shower, antiseptic cream for my hand, and a bed." They had all those things at the Ritz. "I'll deal with the rest in the morning."

"After you talk to Mr. Brown, you can have all those things. I'll even join you in bed."

"In your dreams." And sometimes in mine. But he didn't need to know that.

"I rescued you."

"I rescued me. You drove." Although, I had to give him credit for showing up.

I closed my eyes—just for a few more seconds. Why had he shown up alone? Surely my being kidnapped by terrorists deserved more than one agent. My hand rose to my throat.

"The tracker—"

"What about it?" He sounded defensive.

Working my way up to righteous indignation was diffi-cult. Jake had found me thanks to the tracker. "You told me you took it out."

"I did. Then I put it back."

"Did Mr. Brown know?"

Jake shifted his gaze away. "Strictly speaking, no."

"You tracked me without his knowledge or consent. Or mine." I let go of my locket and closed my fingers around the door handle.

Faster than I would have thought possible, Jake reached across me, stopping me from opening the door. "Mr. Brown thinks I lack objectivity when it comes to you."

Jake was so close I could smell his shampoo and the scent of his skin.

I swallowed. "Does he?" The words came out as a croak.

"And he's right."

I rolled my eyes. A woman could only be lied to so many times. And Jake had reached his quota.

He released the door handle and took my hand. His skin was warm and slightly rough and somehow comforting.

"We were good together, Poppy."

Heat from remembering exactly how good rose to my cheeks. When Jake had been good, he'd been very, very good. And when he'd been bad—well, he'd shattered my heart.

I wasn't over him. Not yet. And here we were. In Paris. In the middle of the night. If I wasn't careful, he'd worm his way back into my heart.

No way was I giving him the power to hurt me a second time. I opened the car door and slowly, painfully, lowered my feet to the pavement.

"Are you hurt?" Jake crouched next to me.

How had he made it around the car that fast?

"Just stiff."

When I stood, he wrapped an arm around my waist, offering his strength. "Let's get you inside. This way."

Leaning on Jake, the warmth of his arm, the sun-kissed scent of him—it was like finding my way home after being lost in a frozen wasteland. Giving in to him would be so easy. Until the pain came. I pulled away. "You should probably grab that laptop."

I walked into the agency's safe house on my own.

When Jake said safe house, I'd conjured up a nondescript house with industrial carpet, furniture left over from the eighties, and the smell of old dust.

The reality was an elegant home. The floors were chevroned oak. The furniture was Empire. And somewhere, someone was burning one of Jo Malone's Peony and Blush Suede candles. The delicate fragrance perfumed the air.

"In here, Miss Fields."

I followed Mr. Brown's voice into a formal salon.

He sat on a fauteuil covered in a delicate damask.

Thor was pacing the back of the room like a caged lion. He stopped when he saw me. He growled when he saw Jake.

That they knew each other came as no surprise.

That Jake stiffened at Thor's growl was even less of a surprise.

"Please—" Mr. Brown waved at a chair that matched his own "—sit down, Poppy. Coffee?"

I collapsed onto the chair. "Water, please."

Thor disappeared through a door, the sound of his footsteps on the parquet fading as he put distance between us.

Jake set the slightly mangled, slightly bloody laptop on the coffee table in front of the empty sofa, then leaned against the wall with his arms and his ankles crossed.

The war of emotions crossing Mr. Brown's fastidious face was fascinating to watch. He desperately wanted to know what secrets the computer held, but he didn't want to touch its less-than-pristine casing. "That needs to go to tech."

"It can wait for a few minutes." Jake bit out.

The two men stared at each other in some kind of manly pissing contest I didn't understand.

Didn't Jake work for Mr. Brown?

Or had he lied to me about that too?

Thor returned to the salon carrying a tray, which he placed on the table next to me. He hadn't brought me a glass of water. He'd brought me a large bottle of Perrier, a crystal goblet filled with ice, and a small plate covered with neatly sliced limes.

"Thank you." Gratitude reached from my hair follicles to my toenails as he poured mineral water over ice.

I looked at the plate of limes, then at my filthy hands.

"Let me." Thor squeezed lime into the water and presented me with the glass.

"What's that sound?" asked Mr. Brown.

I knew precisely what that sound was. Jake was grinding his teeth.

My feelings of gratitude grew and I smiled up at Thor. "Thanks."

"My pleasure."

The grinding grew louder.

Mr. Brown waited until I'd swallowed a few restorative sips of sparkling water. "You saw Badawi?"

"Yes."

"You're sure it was him?"

"He looked exactly like the picture on the FBI site."

"Tell me what happened."

"The taxi driver delivered me to two of Badawi's men— somewhere near Montparnasse. They took me to…" I had no idea where I'd been.

"An industrial storage unit in Sevran," Jake supplied.

"And Badawi was there?"

"No. But he arrived not long after I did."

"Was he alone?"

"He arrived with two men."

"What did they look like?"

"One was tall. He had a thin face, a beard, and a hooked nose. The other guy was shorter and heavier. He had bushy eyebrows and a mustache."

"That's it?"

"You could sit me down with a sketch artist but yeah—that's it. There wasn't anything all that memorable about them."

Mr. Brown drummed his fingers on the arm of his chair. "What did Badawi want with you?"

"He wanted to know what happened to his nephew."

A furrow wrinkled Mr. Brown's brow and he leaned forward, resting his elbows on his knees. "And you told him? The whole story?"

"I did."

He sat back with a jerk as if I'd just whacked at him with a laptop. "He'll go after Diaz."

"You say that like it's a bad thing."

"Why do you think I've asked you to cozy up to Lambert? We're following the Sinaloans' money trail, Ms. Fields." His scowl looked as if it sprang from a deep well of annoyance. "If Diaz dies, the new leader could change everything."

I hadn't considered that. I'd thought Badawi going after Diaz would be a good thing. One bad guy taking out another. "If you were better at sharing information, I would have known that. And—" I leveled a tired gaze at my boss "—if I'd known, I wouldn't have told Badawi the truth."

This situation was not my fault. Mr. Brown had only himself to blame.

"You told me to get close to Ghislain Lambert. You never told me your endgame. And we never discussed terrorists."

Thor claimed the sofa across from me, so I saw the corner of his mouth twitch.

Besides, we had bigger problems than a money trail that

might go cold. "Jake told you Badawi's men were building bombs?" It wasn't exactly a question. If I were to actually ask a question, it would be about why we were talking about Javier Diaz when Badawi was planning an attack on Paris. "What are we going to do?"

"You killed the men who might have been able to tell us more about the attack."

"At the time, I didn't know they were planning an attack and I didn't have much choice. They were going to rape and murder me."

"You killed one of them with a pen."

"It was the closest weapon available."

Thor made a noise that sounded suspiciously like a swallowed bark of laughter.

Jake looked down at his feet as his shoulders shook.

Mr. Brown's scowl deepened.

"It was on the corner of the desk. I couldn't reach the needle-nose pliers." Maybe being a smartass wasn't the wisest choice, but I really was tired and, out of nowhere, I needed a bathroom. Badly.

"You created a situation."

I stood. "So my getting killed would have been the better choice?"

"Where are you going?" Mr. Brown demanded.

"Bathroom."

"Down the hall on the right," said Thor.

"Thanks."

I took off down the hallway, making it to the bathroom just in time.

I washed the grit and blood off my hands, then faced the mirror.

My hair stood out from my head in a tangled mess. My mascara was smudged and tears I didn't know I'd cried had left streaks on my cheeks. All the black I was wearing made me look impossibly pale. No—that was wrong—I didn't *look* impossibly. I *was* impossibly pale. Being drugged, kidnapped, and killing two men will do that to a girl.

I splashed some water on my face, wiping away the raccoon eyes and the tracks of my tears. I raked my fingers through my hair. I straightened my clothes. Then I headed back to the lion's den.

No one had moved. Mr. Brown, looking like a mid-level accountant with a mild case of indigestion, still sat in the fauteuil. Thor, his handsome face arranged into a mask of indifference, still lounged on the couch. Jake, his arms and ankles still crossed, held up the wall.

"We've decided," said Mr. Brown.

"Oh? On what?"

"We need to work quickly."

I looked more closely at Jake. His mouth was a thin line and anger rose off of him like steam. On closer inspection, Thor didn't look any happier. Whatever Mr. Brown had in mind couldn't be good. "Work quickly on what?"

"Getting the information we need from Lambert."

For an instant, everything within me stopped. I couldn't have heard him correctly. "Information? From Lambert?"

Mr. Brown responded with a short, curt nod.

"What are we going to do about the potential bombers?"

Mr. Brown didn't react. "This isn't our country."

Were financial accounts really more important to him than the people who might be killed in another attack on Paris?

"What are we going to do?" I insisted.

"We'll inform la Surêté."

My gaze landed on the laptop. "You're giving them the computer?"

Mr. Brown stretched his legs. "Of course."

I didn't believe him. My face must have reflected my doubt because he clarified. "We'll take a look at what's on it, then turn it over."

That I believed. "How long will looking take? The attack could be tomorrow."

"Ms. Fields, my job is to look out for the United States' interests first."

"Stopping an attack on an ally's soil is in our best interest."

"If there's anything salvageable on that machine—" he wrinkled his nose "— pertaining to imminent attacks, I'll inform French authorities immediately."

Thor gave me a tiny nod.

What did it say that I trusted Thor more than my boss?

It wasn't as if I knew anything about terrorism. I couldn't stop the attacks on my own. I had to trust the people who were trained to handle threats like Badawi's. I sank onto a chair. "What do you want me to do about Lambert?"

"We need access to his computer. If you can get us access, even for a moment, we can clone it."

"So I have to go back into his apartment?"

"Yes."

"I'd have to sneak upstairs."

Mr. Brown nodded. "If that's what it takes."

Ghislain Lambert's computer was on the second floor in the office next to his bedroom. "So, your plan is what? For me to spend the night with him, sneak into his home office while he's sleeping, and do something to his computer?"

Thor looked as if he wanted to hurl a hammer at Mr. Brown's head.

Jake was grinding his teeth again.

Was this the reason Mr. Brown had hired me? To bed men who had information he wanted? Revulsion rumbled through my stomach and I tightened my hands into fists. "Have you ever asked a man to go to bed with a woman as part of a mission?"

Mr. Brown's gaze slid toward Jake.

Shame, scalding and total, washed over me. "How could I forget?"

Jake pushed away from the wall, his lips parted as if he was about to say something.

Whatever it was, I didn't want to hear it. "Fine. I'll do it. I'll get you access to Lambert's computer."

Mr. Brown laced his fingers behind his neck. "Thank you."

I side-eyed Jake. He looked sick—absolutely green.

Good.

I didn't tell either of them I had no intention of going to bed with Ghislain Lambert. There had to be another way. I would find it.

THIRTEEN

"C'mon." Jake held up a key fob. "I'll take you back to Paris."

I stood. Slowly. Every muscle in my body ached and a dull throbbing in my brain pressed against my skull.

I wobbled.

Both Jake and Thor lunged toward me.

Thor reached me first. He took my elbow, propping me upright until my legs steadied. Then he walked me to the car and helped me into the passenger seat. Without a word, he took the seat behind me.

Jake slid behind the wheel and pulled out of the courtyard. To our right, the lights of La Defense sparkled like golden jewels. To our left was Paris.

"Paris is an odd city," Jake observed.

I closed my eyes. "How so?"

"The business center isn't actually in the city."

I could have told him why. Chariss's director boyfriend had gone on for hours at a time about how Paris was the most beautiful city in the world because Parisians had kept (with the exception of Tour Montparnasse) skyscrapers out of the city. "What would you have them tear down to make room for office buildings?"

"There are skyscrapers in London," he replied.

"London was bombed. Paris wasn't."

"Oh. Right."

I glanced back at La Defense and saw Thor's grin. Apparently, me taking Jake down a peg amused him.

There was too much testosterone in the car.

I crossed my arms and stared straight out the windshield. "I've been meaning to thank you."

Jake smirked. "You're welcome."

"What are you thanking him for?" Thor asked.

Men. Thor should be grateful too. Jake had saved us both. "After the party at Ghislain's, he shot at the men who were following us."

Thor looked blank.

"On the quai."

The blank look remained.

"You were there in the car with me and Viktor."

Jake's smirk faded. "That wasn't me."

"What do you mean it wasn't you?" I rubbed the space between my brows. "Who was it?"

"No idea."

"There had to have been video."

"Yeah, there was." Jake flexed his fingers, then tightened them around the wheel. "A guy on a motorcycle toting some major firepower. He took out the guys in the car and rode off. There were no shots of his face. Nothing."

"That doesn't make any sense."

In the backseat, Thor grumbled his agreement.

"Could it have been Badawi's men? He wanted me alive." At least until he'd had a chance to talk to me.

"Maybe you have a guardian angel," Jake suggested.

"Guardian angel?" Thor sounded almost amused.

"Just be glad someone showed up," said Jake. "From what I hear, you and Stone were in serious trouble."

Thor growled.

Jake's eyes narrowed. "If you'd been doing your job, she wouldn't have been in danger."

"It wasn't his fault. No one expected that. No one."

"Maybe if you hadn't lost the killer in the first place," Thor's voice rumbled over us.

Jake's face looked as if it was hewn from granite.

"Diaz wanted me dead before Badawi could get to me."

"Huh?" Thor didn't know the details of my trip to Mexico.

I gave him the SparkNotes version. "When I was in Mexico, I was kidnapped by a drug lord who was obsessed with my mother. While I was being held, another cartel attacked. Lots of people were killed, including Badawi's nephew. He wanted to know who was responsible." I glanced out the window. "Now that I've told him, maybe he'll leave me alone." I crossed my fingers in my lap. "Now that I've shared Diaz's secret, maybe he'll call off the hit. There's no longer any point in killing me."

Both men snorted. It seemed the only thing they could agree on was disagreeing with me.

"Diaz is not calling off any contracts," said Jake.

"Agreed," said Thor.

I stared straight ahead. The Arc de Triomphe glowed in the distance.

I felt Jake's gaze on my face. He reached over and patted my hand. "We need to talk about you and Ghislain Lambert."

I moved my hand out of his reach. "Oh?"

"Brown's plan sucks."

Thor snorted his agreement.

They were right. Mr. Brown's plan did suck, but it was the only plan we had. "Getting close to Ghislain Lambert is the reason I came to Paris."

"You did not come to Paris to seduce a sleazy banker."

"I came to Paris to make a difference. If spending the night with Ghislain is what it takes, so be it." No way was I hopping into bed with Ghislain. No way. I'd sooner sleep with Ja—my brain shied away from that thought.

"You could drug him."

Drug him? Was Jake serious?

"Slip something in his drink." Jake nodded his head as if he'd come up with a brilliant solution.

"That could kill him. And if it didn't, he'd know the next morning."

"You can't go to bed with that guy. Having sex is way outside your job description."

"You went to bed with me."

Thor made a choking sound.

I was over talking about this. Especially with an audience. "Just drop it, okay? It's none of your business."

"It is my business."

"It is not."

"Where should I take you?" Jake's voice was wintry, a sure sign I'd made him mad.

"The Ritz."

"Anywhere we can grab a taxi," said Thor. "We don't want anyone running these plates."

We drove the rest of the way into Paris in chilly silence.

Jake took us to Maison Souquet, a hotel that began its life as a brothel.

Maybe Thor missed Jake's point. I did not.

When I got out of the car, I slammed the door extra hard.

A moment later, Thor and I were in a taxi.

"Do you want to talk about it?" he asked.

"About what?" I snapped. There were so many things I didn't want to talk about. I'd ignored his warning and hopped into a car with men who'd ultimately wanted to kill me. I'd killed two people. I'd agreed to seduce a man I hardly knew (there had to be a way around that). I'd had a fight with Jake.

"I'm just trying to be helpful."

I felt a pang of guilt. The man was trying to be nice and I'd nearly bitten off his head.

"Talking's not my thing right now."

"Got it." He leaned his head against the seat rest and kept his mouth shut.

I did the same.

Miraculously, there were no photographers camped in front of the Ritz.

We slipped through the lobby and upstairs to the suite.

I was exhausted but too wired too sleep. "I don't know about you, but I could use a drink." I opened the cabinet concealing the bar.

"Yeah. Sure."

"What'll it be?"

"Bourbon. Neat."

I poured two.

I handed Thor his drink and sank onto the sofa. "How did you get involved in all this?"

"You needed a bodyguard."

"Before that. How did you come to work for Mr. Brown?"

Thor glanced at Chariss's closed door.

"She's out cold. Guaranteed." Chariss had insomnia. When she was working, she took pills to help her sleep. In between projects, she worked out till she dropped.

"Recruited out of special forces."

I nodded. "My dad was special forces."

"Wha—"

Thunk.

The noise came from my room.

Thor brought a single finger to his lips, then motioned for me to stay on the couch.

Not likely.

He tiptoed across the room.

"It was probably Consuela." I got off the couch and tiptoed after him.

Thor turned, saw me, and rolled his eyes. "No way that little dog made that big of a sound. Don't forget, Diaz's hitmen are still out there." One hand closed on the doorknob, the other gripped his gun.

Using the muzzle he pushed the door open.

"*Eeek!*" The scream from my bedroom was almost loud enough to pierce Chariss's drug-induced stupor.

"Shut up!" I whispered furiously.

"He's pointing a gun at me!"

"Mark, this is Mia."

Thor lowered his gun and stared. I couldn't blame him. Mia was nearly naked.

"Mia, this is Mark."

Mia stared back. It wasn't every day a woman met Thor.

"What are you doing here?" I demanded.

She blinked. Slowly. "I came to see you."

"Why are you in my bedroom?" It was perfectly obvious Mia had been sleeping in my bed. But why?

"I was tired."

"Yes, but why my room?"

"Consuela didn't want to be alone."

Consuela lifted her chin off her paws and yawned.

Mia snatched my robe off the bottom of the bed and slipped it on. "You're the bodyguard?"

"Yeah." Thor looked more dazed than the long day or shot of bourbon warranted.

My best friend frequently turned men into gibbering idiots. Why should Thor be immune?

"You know what? I'm exhausted. I'm going to bed." I pushed into my bedroom. "Good night, Mark." I closed the door and turned on Mia. "What are you doing here?"

"I told you. I was worried. You made international news."

I scrubbed my face with my palms. "That's nice of you, bu—"

"The hotel is fully booked. They don't have a room for me

until tomorrow. Chariss said you wouldn't mind sharing for one night."

"I don't. I'm just surprised."

"Your mother said your guard was totally gorgeous."

"Stay away from him." My voice was sharper than was strictly necessary.

Mia's brows rose. "You have dibs?"

"No. You get interested in a man and he doesn't see anyone but you. I need him watching my back. When this is over and no one's trying to kill me, you can do what you want."

"If I were you, I'd call dibs."

Jake had trampled my heart so thoroughly I doubted I'd be interested in another man for at least a decade. "Just wait, okay? I'm going to take a shower."

"Good idea. You sort of smell."

Consuela growled, saving me the trouble.

When I emerged from the shower, Mia was asleep. On my side of the bed.

I swallowed a sigh and climbed between the sheets. I was out before my head touched the pillow.

Yip, yip, yip.

I pried my eyes open to a bedroom bathed in light.

Yip, yip, yip.

"Aren't you just the cutest?" Whoever was talking to Consuela wasn't making a good impression. Then again, it was hard to impress Consuela.

My hand fumbled for my phone on the bedside table until I remembered it had been smashed to pieces. What a pain. I picked up the hotel line and ordered a fresh pot of coffee to be delivered as soon as possible.

Mia was gone. She'd left shoes, the tiny T-shirt she'd worn to bed, and countless pieces of luggage strewn about the room.

If the Ritz didn't have a room today, she was moving to the George V or the Peninsula. I couldn't live like this.

I swung my legs out of bed, inventoried my aches and pains, and decided some ibuprofen could handle them all.

A few minutes later, I emerged into the living room, where Consuela was watching Dylan Roberts. There was a snarl frozen on the dog's little face—an expression that usually resulted in me apologizing to someone.

I scooped Consuela into my arms.

André and Mia were helping themselves to pastries and Thor was in his usual spot, watching Place Vendôme from the window.

"Where's Chariss?" I asked.

"She left already." Mia picked up the last croissant and bit into it.

André wrapped his arms around me. "I haven't seen you since that awful car chase."

"Yesterday was a busy day."

He cast a quick glance at Thor. "I bet."

I didn't want to talk about my need for a bodyguard. "How were the catacombs?"

"Terrifying." André shuddered.

"But we love your idea." Dylan emptied the last of the coffee into her cup. "The one for urban exploring."

"Is that a fresh pot?"

"No," André hurried to assure me. "Should I order more?"

"Already on its way." I should have ordered pastries as well.

"We were wondering if—"

Tap, tap.

Thor shifted his attention to the door.

"That's probably my coffee."

He grunted and crossed the room. "Who is it?"

"Room service."

Thor opened the door and a bellhop with a fresh pot of coffee wafted into the suite.

"On the table please," I waved toward the coffee table. "Would you please ask the kitchen to send up another basket of bread? All croissants?"

"Of course, Mademoiselle Fields." The young man picked up the empty coffee pot and left us.

I set Consuela down and poured myself a cup of coffee, pausing to breathe in its aroma.

"As I was saying—"

"Dylan, let's let Poppy drink her coffee before we bother her."

I glanced André's way. Whatever Dylan had to say, I wasn't going to like it.

Brnng, brnng.

I picked up the phone. "Hello."

"A call for you, Mademoiselle Fields. A Monsieur Lambert."

"I'll take it."

"How long are you staying?" André asked Mia.

I waved them quiet. "Hello."

"Poppy, c'est Ghislain au telephone."

"Good morning."

"I'm calling to see if you'll have dinner with me tonight."

"I'd love to, but—"

Thor regarded me with unreadable eyes.

"But what?"

"I'm not eating in public until the person who's trying to kill me is caught."

"That is nothing. I'll cook for you. At my apartment."

This was what Mr. Brown wanted. "Then I'd love to. What time?"

"Eight o'clock?"

"Perfect. We'll be there."

"We?"

"Me and my guard."

"My apartment is perfectly safe." I could prick myself on the sharp point of Ghislain's voice. "You don't need a guard."

I glanced Thor's way. "He can wait in the foyer, but I can't come without him."

"Very well." Ghislain's annoyance was obvious.

"*A bientôt.*" *See you soon.*

I hung up the phone and looked at Thor. "Eight o'clock."

"I heard."

"Tonight."

He nodded.

"Tonight?" Dylan's voice held a plaintive note.

"Is there a problem?" What possible objection could Dylan have to my going on a date?She flashed me one of her super-bright smiles. "André and I were hoping you'd help us scout locations in the catacombs."

"Are you out of your mind?" Mia tilted her head to the side as if she genuinely wondered if Dylan was nuts. "You do know that someone's trying to kill Poppy? Right?"

Dylan held out her hands to me. "The tape would be so much better if you were on it."

Unbelievable. I looked at André.

He responded with a what-am-I-gonna-do shrug.

"*Grrr.*" Consuela didn't think much of Dylan's idea either.

Mia gave Dylan the dirtiest look in her repertoire. "She's not going."

"I don't think the catacombs are a great idea right now." Security would be a nightmare.

"Duh." Mia obviously didn't care if she offended André's client.

Dylan kept smiling. "It's just—"

"Not helping, Dylan." At least André sounded kind. "I'm sure if she could, Poppy would help."

"She's going out on a date, but she can't spend an hour in the catacombs?" Dylan pointed at Thor. "She can bring him."

Like Mia, Thor glared at Dylan. "Miss Fields' safety is the top priority."

Now Dylan's smile faded. "But—"

"It's impossible." Thor's voice was a door slamming shut.

Now a sneer curled Dylan's lips. "Oh, please. Poppy Fields does exactly what she wants, when she wants. She could make it work. She just doesn't want to help me."

I didn't have the energy for this. "Dylan, it's fairly easy to protect me in a private home. The catacombs present a challenge."

"Bull. You're too selfish to help me."

I stared at her. Was she on drugs? What was wrong with her?

"You don't think I'm good enough. Don't think I didn't see those smirks when I ordered a lemon drop martini."

"You ordered a lemon drop?" Mia covered her lips with her fingers. "In a club?"

"Not helping." André poked Mia in the ribs. "Dylan, Poppy's life is more important than a reality show."

Dylan slammed down her cup, sloshing coffee onto the table top. She hitched her handbag onto her shoulder and marched to the door. "Are you coming, André?"

"No."

She stared at him for a long second, then stormed out.

"What is wrong with that woman?" Mia demanded.

André shrugged and reached for a palmier. "Not sure, but she needs a new agent."

FOURTEEN

Spending the day at the Ritz should have been restful. I was in a luxurious suite with access to gourmet food and a world-renowned spa.

Chariss was on set, André had dashed off for a meeting, and Thor, having secured my promise not to set so much as a toe in the hallway, had gone to pick up a new phone for me.

That left Mia, who was immune to luxury, on a diet, and not in a spa mood.

She curled up in a corner of the couch and insisted we talk.

"Why does someone want you dead?" She leveled a scowl my direction. "Does this have something to do with what happened in Mexico?" Mia might look like some hippy-dippy flower child, but she was as sharp they came.

"Yes."

Her brow creased with worry. "I'm glad you've got Mark to protect you." She wrapped a strand of hair around her index finger and shifted her gaze to Consuela. "When I read there had been two attempts on your life, I had to come. I'll never forgive myself for leaving you alone in Mexico."

There was a reason Mia was my best friend. We might

differ on little things, but when big stuff came along, she was always there. "Staying in Cabo wouldn't have made a differ-ence. I felt better knowing you were safe. Besides, everything turned out okay."

She narrowed her eyes and fisted her hands. "It's not okay. Not at all. Some Sinaloan drug lord is trying to kill you. It's. Not. Okay."

It was a good thing she didn't know about the kidnapping attempts.

Consuela, who was curled in my lap, opened one eye as if she were curious about what I'd say next.

I could take care of myself (sort of), and I had Thor to protect me. "I'll be fine." I added a dash of confidence I didn't feel. "Just fine."

"You need me."

Mia, who was so thin a strong wind could lift her off her feet, wouldn't be much help if an assassin made another attempt on my life. Quite the opposite. But her heart was in the right place.

"I'll be fine." If the dubious expression on her face was any indication, repetition did not make me more convincing.

"Pfft." Mia held out her hand and checked the glossiness of her manicure. "Who's this guy you're going out with?" Her pretended disinterest wasn't fooling anyone.

"His name is Ghislain Lambert. He's a banker."

"A banker? You're risking your life to go out with a banker?"

"Would risking my life to go out with a male model be any better?"

"Maybe if his father was a Greek shipping magnate."

"Ha."

"Maybe if he could make you forget about Jake."

We were not talking about Jake. "Ghislain is charming and handsome and I think he might be hiding a title in his closet." Also, I was going to compromise his computer.

She wrinkled her nose. "Hardly seems worth the risk. French counts are a dime a dozen."

"I can't spend my life hiding."

"That's not what you told Dylan."

Ugh. "It really would be hard to keep me safe in the catacombs. Ghislain lives in an apartment overlooking the Seine. I'll be fine."

"I'll worry."

"Nothing will happen." I crossed my fingers behind my back. I'd gain access to the computer. Ghislain would never know. We would not have sex.

"I could come with you. I'll be Mark's date."

"Mark is my bodyguard and Ghislain knows it."

Mia leaned her head back and sighed. "He looks like Chris Hemsworth."

"I'm aware."

"What am I going to do tonight?"

"Go out with André."

"He'll be in a mood. He always is when he loses a client."

"He may not be too sorry about this one."

"Why did he take her on in the first place? Isn't she a season or two past her shelf life?" Most reality stars had a limited amount of time to capitalize on their fame.

"No idea." I wasn't about to share André's secret.

"But you can guess. I can tell from your expression."

That was the problem with Mia. She could read me too easily.

"My guess is that Dylan has an investor lined up for this reality show."

"So? There's something else you're not telling me. Spill." Stubborn could learn a few things from Mia.

"I can't tell you. André asked me to keep his secret."

"From me? We both know he'll tell me."

She was right. He would tell her.

"Then you'd better ask him."

With a dramatic roll of her eyes, she texted, her fingers flying across the screen.

A moment later she looked up, a stunned expression on her face. "André? Produce?"

André, Mia, and I made a point of avoiding paths blazed by our famous parents. André's father was a golden-boy producer until one of his projects flopped. Mia's father was a country singer immediately recognizable by his first name. And Chariss—Chariss was Chariss.

Mia shook her head. "What's next? Are you going to start acting?"

"Right after you release an album."

Color rose to her cheeks.

"You didn't!"

"Dad wanted me to try. Just for fun. To see if I liked the process."

"Country?"

She looked down at her hands. "Coffeehouse."

"When do I get to hear it?"

Her blush deepened.

"When?" I insisted.

"We're not talking about me. We're talking about your safety."

"That's Mark's job. And you didn't answer my question."

"Soon."

"How soon?"

She shrugged, grabbed the remote, and turned on the television. "Who's that?"

I glanced at the screen. A face—high forehead, prominent cheekbones, deep-set eyes, and thin lips—looked out at me. "Marcel Charbeau."

"Who?"

"Marcel Charbeau. He's a politician."

"Why is he so pissed off?"

"I think that's his usual expression. He's more of a nationalist than the nationalists."

"What does that mean?"

"He's all about France for the French. He doesn't like Muslims and disagrees with France's immigration policies. He says the end of France is imminent due to differing birthrates."

Mia looked at me with a blank expression. "Huh?"

"Birthrates among Muslim families are higher than the rest of the population. With changing demographics, Charbeau believes France will change. And not for the better."

"Oh." She changed the channel. "How do you know all that?"

A ruffled copy of *Le Figaro* still lay on the coffee table. "I read." Not for a second did I believe Mia cared about French politics. "You're stalling. I want to hear about your album."

She picked up a copy of French *Vogue*. "Tell you what, you come back safe from your date and I'll play it for you."

THOR and I sat side by side in the back of a taxi. Traffic wasn't moving, and Thor stared out at the Seine as if the river were to blame.

"Ghislain doesn't expect me to be on time."

"Oh?"

"He expects me to keep him waiting."

Thor nodded once and looked over his shoulder.

"He'll also expect me to treat you like hired help."

"No problem." The scowl on Thor's face said the opposite.

"If he thinks I brought a friend, there's no way he'll take me upstairs."

The scowl deepened. "I get it."

"You know, being seduced by Ghislain Lambert wasn't on my list of things to do in Paris."

"Yeah." Satisfied there were no threats behind us, he turned and looked at me. "What's your plan?"

"I'll do whatever it takes to get access to his computer."

Thor snorted.

"What?"

"You don't strike me as the kind of woman who takes sex lightly. You're not going to bed with that guy. What's your plan?"

Thor had known me two days and he understood me better than Jake. "My plan is to wing it." It was a terrible plan.

My turn to look out the window. The Hôtel de Ville was bathed in golden light and looked more like a palace built for a fairy princess than the seat of the Parisian government. "Getting those account numbers from Ghislain Lambert could mean freezing billions of dollars in assets. It could mean the end of the Sinaloan Cartel."

"And?"

"The cartel exports misery to the United States."

Thor touched my arm. Lightly.

I turned my gaze to him.

"If the Sinaloan Cartel crumbles, another cartel will take its place."

"That's very cynical." I couldn't think that. Could not. Ending a drug cartel had to make a difference.

"That's the truth. Do you know who Zhenli Ye Gon is?"

"No."

"He's a Chinese-born Mexican who worked for the Sinaloans and imported the chemicals needed to make meth. When the Mexican police raided his house, they found more than two hundred million dollars in cash." He paused, letting the figure sink into my psyche. "The loss of that money and his arrest were a blip for the Sinaloans."

"You're saying I can't make a difference?" I'd show him. I'd march into Ghislain's, I'd load the damned clone on his computer, and Mr. Brown would have the information he needed to take down Diaz.

"You look angry."

"No, I don't." Maybe I did.

"I'm not saying you can't make a difference. You definitely can. Just don't compromise who you are. Not for this."

"It's too late to turn back now."

"No." His hand touched my arm again. "It isn't."

The taxi slowed to a stop in front of Ghislain's building.

"You don't have to do this," said Thor.

"Yes—" I opened the car door "—I do." I had things to prove—to myself.

Thor followed me into Ghislain's building. "Poppy—"

What now?

"I've got your back."

My nerves, which I thought I had under control, leapt as soon as I saw the Frenchman. I smiled and covered the trembling of my lips with a wide smile.

"Come in." Ghislain pulled me into his home.

Thor came with me.

Ghislain's narrowed his eyes and stared at him. The Frenchman's handsome face looked a lot less handsome when he pouted.

"Someone is trying to kill me. He can do a quick walk-through, then wait someplace out of the way."

Thor checked Ghislain's apartment for hidden killers, found none, and took up a position just inside the front door.

"He can wait outside."

Thor shook his head—a tiny but definitive movement.

"He won't bother us. I promise." I rested my hand on Ghislain's arm and fluttered my lashes. "I'd feel safer with him in the apartment."

The petulant thrust of my host's lower lip confirmed what I already knew. I could not go to bed with him. I wasn't a good enough actress.

"Fine."

We left Thor in the foyer.

Ghislain led me to the salon with the killer view. "Wine?"

"Please."

"Red or white?"

"Whatever you're drinking." Ghislain had expensive taste in wine, but it wouldn't matter what he served me. My stomach was in knots. No way could I swallow even a sip.

"*Une minute.*" He disappeared into the kitchen.

Now I really wasn't drinking whatever he poured. A friend—a naïve friend, who didn't watch her drink being poured—ended up in a sex tape. Ghislain could slip anything into my glass. Or maybe I was being paranoid.

If I was actually trained, what would I do?

I'd climb into Ghislain's bed, wait until he fell asleep, and sneak into his office like some stealth shadow.

I steeled my resolve.

I even smiled at Ghislain when he returned carrying two glasses.

He gave one to me. "To the most beautiful woman in Paris."

"*Merci.*" We touched our glasses together and I put my lips on the rim but didn't swallow.

Ghislain had no qualms about the wine. He drank deeply. "What did you do today?"

"My friend, Mia, is in Paris and I spent the morning with her. This afternoon, she went shopping and I went to the Chanel Spa at the Ritz. What about you?" I sat down on a sofa, leaving room for him to join me.

Ghislain sat close enough for our thighs to brush together.

He put his wine glass on the table. "I dealt with pain-in-the-ass Asian clients all afternoon. I assure you, your afternoon at the spa was preferable."

I put my glass down next to his and smiled at him as if

he'd just recounted the most fascinating story ever. "What was so awful about them?"

"Paris is being overrun. The Arabs have bought up most of Ile St. Louis. The island is a second-home enclave for them. Almost all the businesses on the island have gone out of business because there are no actual residents." He pulled at the collar of his shirt. "There are lines of Chinese waiting to get into Louis Vuitton. Northern Paris looks like a suburb of Islamabad."

"France for the French?"

"We'll make an exception for beautiful Americans." He crossed his ankle over his knee. "Tell me about yourself."

"I'm an open book. I want to know more about you. Where did you grow up?"

"Mostly in Paris."

"What were you like as a little boy?" I leaned forward and claimed Ghislain's glass as my own. Perhaps he didn't notice because his gaze was locked on the deep vee of my sweater.

"I was a typical boy. I liked fútbol and pretty girls." An oily smile settled on his lips. "Not much has changed."

"But you became a banker, not a soccer star."

"I was not meant to play for France. Banking seemed a better way to pay the bills."

I looked around the palatial apartment and let my eyes widen. "You said this place belonged to a client. Where do you live?" Which client?

"I haven't bought an apartment yet. I'm thinking about something in the sixteenth arrondissement."

Hardly a surprise.

We talked. I drank his wine. He drank mine.

Something dinged in the kitchen and Ghislain staggered to his feet.

Seriously?

He really had dropped something in my wine?

He rubbed his eyes with the back of one hand and

clutched the back of a chair with the other. "I'd better check dinner."

He took three steps and collapsed to the chevroned floor boards like a soufflé tapped by a spoon.

The man was out cold.

"Thor!" Not surprisingly, Mark did not come running.

"Mark!"

That got an immediate response. Thor appeared in the doorway to the salon and took in Ghislain's inert body. "What the hell happened?"

"He tried to drug me."

"And?" He narrowed his eyes. "What did you do?"

"I switched our glasses."

Thor snickered.

I glanced toward the stairs that led to the second floor. "What should we do with him?"

"Leave him there. He meant to do this to you."

Tempting. "At least put him on the couch. I'll see if he left his computer on." I crossed my fingers and climbed the stairs to the second floor.

The computer screen in Ghislain's office glowed softly in the darkness and I breathed a sigh of relief.

Ghislain's chair beckoned.

I settled behind the desk and pushed a button. The computer's screen came to life and I typed in the site Mr. Brown told me to visit. While I waited, I shuffled through the papers on the desk. A list of Paris locales with times sifted to the top of the stack.

Gare du Nord: 13:00

Pompidou: 13:30

Les Deux Magots: 14:00

Sacré-Couer: 14:30

Le Tour Eiffel: 15:00

The busiest train station in Europe, a center that attracted artists, students, and families, a famous café frequented almost exclusively by tourists, a basilica, and the Eiffel Tower —why did Ghislain have them on a list?

Unease tapped me on the shoulder. Was Ghislain up to something worse than cleaning money for drug cartels?

If so, what?

I took out my new phone and clicked a picture of the paper.

"Poppy!" Thor stood in the doorway, and he was whispering. "Are you done?"

I glanced at the screen. "Yeah."

"Good. We've got to get out of here. Now."

FIFTEEN

I pushed away from Ghislain's desk and stood fast enough for the wheeled chair to roll backward. "What happened? What's going on?"

"There are gunmen in the apartment."

I froze, apparently struck stupid by his announcement. "Gunmen? How?"

"Let's go."

But my feet were still rooted. "How many?"

"At least three."

Three? There were three men here to kill me? My mouth went dry. "You have a gun?"

"Of course."

Now, I could hear movement on the floor below us. Tables knocked over. Glass shattered. "Can we shoot our way out?"

"Doubtful."

"Then what are we going to do?"

Thor looked at the window. "Ever done any rappelling?"

We were on the top floor of a seven-story apartment building. "You're kidding."

"I'm not."

"We don't have any rope." It was a reasonable objection.

The other objection—that my intestines liquefied at the thought of rappelling down a building—remained unspoken.

"Sheets."

Visions of plummeting to the ground filled my mind. "That's crazy."

"We don't have to make it all the way to the street. Just to a neighboring building's roof. It's just two stories. And we don't have time to discuss this." Thor left me, ran into Ghislain's bedroom, and yanked the sheets off the bed.

"I hate rappelling."

"You'll like getting shot even less." He glared at the length of the tied-together sheets. "It's not long enough. We need more sheets."

Bang.

I jumped five feet in the air. "What was that?"

"They just executed your date."

Ghislain? We'd left him defenseless on a couch. And now he was dead?

Guilt opened its jaws and sank its teeth deep into my psyche.

Thor snapped his fingers in front of my face. "He wouldn't have been there if he hadn't tried to drug you."

"But he's dead." Because we'd left him alone.

"And we will be too if we don't get out of here."

Something large crashed downstairs.

Maybe climbing down the side of a building wouldn't be so bad.

Or maybe being shot wouldn't be so bad.

Thor dashed into one of the spare bedrooms, pulled the sheets off the bed, and knotted them onto the existing length of sheets. Then he tied one end to the bedframe, tossed the extra length out the window, and pushed the bed across the floor so it wouldn't slide when we escaped. "Go!"

With my heart relocated in my throat, I went.

The breeze that seemed gentle at ground level tugged at me.

My hands practically strangled the linen. If I fell, that was it. I would not look down. I would not. I would concentrate on my hands, and feet, and slowly descending the side of a building.

I could do this. I could. I pushed down the fear gnawing away at my confidence, braced my feet against the building's wall, and took another step.

"Hurry!"

I scowled up at Thor. I was doing my best.

He swung a leg out the window and grabbed a handful of sheet.

Would the tied-together linen hold us both?

I hurried.

Then Thor was fully out the window too.

The sheets could rip or the bed give way or a gunman could shoot down on us. I hurried faster.

"Move to the left."

I scowled up at him. Was he kidding? Going down was hard enough.

But I followed directions. With each inch downward, I moved an inch to the left.

It seemed like forever until my feet touched the neighboring building's roof. In reality only a moment had passed.

Thor dropped the last few feet and landed next to me.

The roof was covered in tiny bits of gravel and a café table and two chairs surrounded by pots of herbs. The scents of rosemary and lavender filled the air. Well, rosemary, lavender, and fear.

Thor didn't seem inclined to admire the herbs. "C'mon." He grabbed my hand and pulled me to the roof-access door.

Locked. Of course.

Thor pointed his gun at the door.

"Wait!"

"What?"

I picked up a lone brick.

"You can't break the lock with that."

"It's not real." I'd been on enough Paris rooftops to know residents hid keys rather than bother their concierge if they got locked out. I slid away the bottom of the fake brick and shook the door key into my palm.

Seconds later we were inside. We made sure the door was locked and raced down the stairs.

My breath came in short pants and a stitch in my side made each step painful, but I kept going. Five flights.

Thor stopped in the foyer. Stopped so suddenly I bumped into him.

"*Oomph.*"

"Shhh."

The sharp, terrifying ping of a bullet meeting metal carried down the stairs.

"They're coming." Gesturing for me to stay back, Thor peered through the glass panel in the front door. "Dammit."

"There's someone out there?"

He nodded. "Yeah." The tone of his *yeah* convinced me the man in the street was armed with at least a rocket launcher.

We were caught between whoever was on their way down those five flights and a man who could blow us to smithereens.

I looked around the foyer. We were trapped in a typical Parisian apartment building. Black and white tile covered the floor, panel molding decorated the walls, and a chandelier with most of its bulbs burned out offered feeble light. The door to the concierge's living quarters was firmly closed. What wasn't typical was a hallway leading to the back of the building. "That way." There had to be a courtyard or a back garden, maybe even an alley or access to the street.

We ran down the hall, pushed through a door, and found cars. The courtyard had been converted to parking.

Cars were a good sign. There had to be an exit.

I drew breath deep into my lungs and searched. There! I pointed to a covered passage just big enough for a horse and carriage. "Let's go."

We ran.

Bang!

The whine of a bullet speeding past my head had me flinging myself to the ground. My knees and elbows met the cobbles. Hard. The rest of me slammed to the ground and all the air in my lungs escaped with one whoosh.

"Get behind the car!" Thor hauled me (gasping for air) to the far side of a Peugeot and fired his Glock at the man who'd shot at us.

In the enclosed courtyard, the echoes of the gunshots were louder than the actual shots themselves. The buildings vibrated with noise and lights in the windows overlooking the courtyard flickered on.

That was good. Surely someone would call the police.

Too bad whoever was stationed on the quai was sure to have heard the shooting. They'd come. Thor and I would be trapped.

I rose into a crouch. "We've got to get out of here." That's what I said. What came out was *ee-ah-oo-eh-ere.*

"What?"

I pointed to the exit.

Thor nodded. "Can you hotwire a car?"

I simply stared at him.

"Never mind." Thor thrust the gun at me. "Hold them off for a minute."

He eased open a car door and, keeping his head low, slid into the vehicle. The grumble of its engine a few seconds later was one of the sweetest sounds I'd ever heard.

Bang!

A bullet pocked the car.

My head swiveled back to the building we'd just escaped. A shadow lurked in the doorway.

In the street, there was shouting.

"Either get in or shoot!" Thor sounded as crazed as Chariss the night when, shortly after I'd moved in with her, Mia and I drove her new Maserati into the Pacific. Chariss seemed to believe there was intent—that I'd drowned her car because I was angry my father's plane had gone down in a fiery ball and I was forced to live with the woman who'd never wanted me. She'd been wrong. The car ending up in the ocean had been an accident. Mostly.

I'd never seen anyone look as angry since. Until now.

Bang!

A bullet shattered the rear window.

I peeked around the frame and spotted the shooter. His shoulders and part of his head were just visible in the doorway to the apartment building. I steadied my hand, aimed, and pulled the trigger.

The man's shoulders crumpled, and he fell.

Thor cut short my stomach's sick, I-just-shot-a-human-being flip. "Get in the car. Now."

I glanced toward the exit to the street. We were too late. A car the size of Texas—too big to fit through the passage but the perfect size to make escape impossible—blocked our way to freedom. And, like a clown car from hell, it seemed to be ejecting an unreasonable number of men. All of them armed, and not with plastic flowers that shot water.

Diaz had hired an army to kill me.

The men opened fire and I flung myself on the cobblestones and covered my head. And ears. The noise was deafening.

So many men. So many guns. Our only hope was that the police arrived quickly. Before there was nothing left of us but bullet holes.

The car Thor had hotwired was worthless. We couldn't drive into a wall of bullets. Not without being shredded.

Thor joined me on the ground. He pulled the gun from my fingers and poked at me, pointing toward an apartment building, where the stone walls might actually stop a bullet or two.

But the building was so far away. We'd never make it.

I shook my head.

His face darkened, and he pointed. Insisting. He risked a peek around the corner of the car and shot.

"Go." His mouth was moving but, with a whole troop of assassins shooting at us, I couldn't hear a word. Especially not that word.

If he thought I'd leave him—let him cover my escape—he was so wrong. I wasn't going anywhere without him.

Having someone die to save me was not on my list of things to do in Paris. I shook my head.

Thor's mouth moved, but the words were lost in the sound of automatic fire.

It didn't matter what he said—what he thought. My running for cover wouldn't make a bit of difference—not when the cars protecting us were being reduced to rubble in a hail of gunfire.

Any second now, one of those bullets would find one of us.

Whomp!

The blast of the explosion pressed me closer to the cobblestones and the air in my lungs burned like fire.

Thor collapsed onto the cobblestones next to me and the look on his face said what I already knew: if the cars around us started exploding, we'd be incinerated. He pushed up to his hands and knees. "Go!"

I looked again at the building and hardened my resolve. Either we went together or not at all.

I kicked at Thor. "You too."

He regarded me with narrowed eyes.

I jerked my chin at our goal, tapped my chest, then pointed at him. "Both of us."

He rolled his eyes. "Fine."

I pulled myself forward on my elbows and forearms. Even as the paving stones bored their way into my elbow bones, I waited for a bullet to rip into my back.

Nothing zinged by me. Nothing.

I looked over my shoulder. Thor, the jackass, hadn't moved. If, by some miracle, we escaped, I'd have a few things to say to him. "Come on!"

The men in the entrance were still shooting—just not at us.

I risked a better look.

The car they'd piled out of was a burned-out wreck and the remaining gunmen were shooting at someone in the street. One man twisted and fell backward. A second man did the same.

The insurmountable army of men had been reduced to two. And those two were fully engaged with whoever was shooting at them.

I raised up into a crouch, returned to Thor, and grabbed his arm. "Let's go!"

"You first."

I'd fallen for that once already. "Not without you."

"Poppy—"

"C'mon." I pulled on his arm.

A bullet whizzed by my ear. Somehow, I'd forgotten about the men in the apartment building.

Thor gave me a look most people reserve for babbling idiots, rose to a crouch, and shot twice.

Two men fell.

He grabbed my upper arm in a death grip and yanked me toward the safety of a building.

That's when I noticed the quiet.

The absence of gunshots was almost as loud as the shots

themselves. The only sounds were my breathing and the distant whine of emergency vehicles' sirens.

Distant

If the police hadn't been shooting at the man blocking the exit from the courtyard, who had?

I shook off Thor's grip (that I could free myself from his iron grasp spoke volumes about the power of adrenaline and Thor's weakened state). Clutching ribs that had met cobbles with far too much force, I limped toward the pile of dead men.

"Poppy!"

I ignored Thor and stumbled into the street.

Traffic was stalled. Smart Parisians had abandoned their cars and taken cover during the gun battle.

No one and nothing was moving except—I squinted into the darkness. A figure climbed onto a motorcycle. As if my gaze had actual weight, the figure turned.

The face was covered by a black helmet, but I felt the gaze. And I sensed fury. Almost as if our rescuer was angry I'd stumbled into the street rather than running for cover.

I took one tentative step forward.

The motorcycle came to life with an evil growl. My guardian angel—the man who was a complete mystery to me —the man who'd saved me twice—turned his back and disappeared into the night.

"Who was that?" Thor stood at my back.

"No idea."

"I owe him."

"We owe him."

He nodded his agreement. "We should get out of here."

How many men were dead? I looked around. Pieces of the destroyed car and bodies littered the sidewalk and street, and the sirens were almost as deafening as the bullets had been.

"Shouldn't we stay? Tell the police what happened?"

"No."

I opened my mouth—

"Please, don't argue. Not now." The exhaustion in his voice had me sealing my lips.

I nodded.

Thor pulled me across the gridlocked quai and down to the Parc des Rives running near the Seine.

My legs shook. My chin quivered.

Thor wrapped his arm around my back and propelled us forward.

To our left, the river ran as it had for millennia. Ahead of us, Notre Dame, nearly eight hundred years old, stood bathed in golden light. If I tried, I'd be able to spot Sainte Chapelle, the chapel built to house Christ's relics.

The river, the cathedral, the chapel—they'd seen much worse than what happened tonight.

"I need to sit down." My voice shook as badly as my legs.

Thor led me to a bench and my legs gave way.

He patted his jacket and pulled out a crushed phone. "Do you have yours?"

I reached into my pocket and pulled out the new phone. Miraculously, it was still in one piece. I handed it over.

"Password?"

I rattled off the numbers.

He raised his brows.

"The day my father died."

He nodded and entered the digits.

"What's this?"

He held out my phone. The picture I'd taken in Ghislain's office glowed in the night.

"It was on Ghislain's desk."

"But what is it?"

"I don't know, but it looked important."

Thor grunted and dialed. "We're maybe a quarter mile from Lambert's. To the west. Near the river." He listened. "She loaded it, but Lambert's dead."

I lowered my head to my hands.

"Not sure, sir. Plenty of hostiles. All dead." He listened again.

I struggled to my feet and limped to the fence overlooking the Seine. I didn't want to hear another word. Instead, I looked out over the water.

I concentrated on the sound of the water. Even so, I heard Thor.

"We'd be dead, but the mystery guy—the one who followed us the last time we were here—he saved us."

SIXTEEN

A taciturn driver loaded Thor and me into a car. "I'm taking you to Neuilly."

I didn't care where the driver took me as long as I could put my feet up. I rested my head against the seat and closed my eyes on the lights of Paris. My arms were too heavy to move and sinking into bed sounded better than anything. Ever.

"What do you know about Dylan Roberts?" Thor asked from the front seat.

I opened one eye. "Not much. She was on that show." The name escaped me.

"What show?"

"You know the one."

"No, I don't."

I struggled for a name. "Think *The Real World* meets *The Bachelor*."

"Not helping."

The driver snorted, saving me the trouble.

"Don't you watch television?" I asked.

"The news."

That Thor didn't spend his days keeping up with Kim and

Khloe wasn't exactly a surprise. But no television? "No Netflix? No Prime?"

"I work."

"You've never binged a show?"

"No."

"Never?" How were we even from the same planet?

"No." Annoyance crept into his voice. "Back to Dylan Roberts."

"Why do you care about Dylan?" Especially right now. We had better things to think about than Dylan and how she'd snagged her fifteen minutes of fame.

"She knew you'd be at Lambert's tonight."

I opened my other eye. One of those bullets had rattled Thor's brain. "You think Dylan Roberts called up Diaz's hit squad and told them where I'd be?" Not in a million years. She wouldn't know the first thing about contacting Diaz.

"I think you were photographed with her and it's possible someone promised her a large payment to let them know your whereabouts in advance."

When he put it that way, Dylan selling me out wasn't nearly as ridiculous. Thor might be right. "It could just as easily have been Ghislain Lambert. I bet he would have betrayed his grandmother if the price was right." Talking ill of a dead man who'd slipped drugs in my drink didn't seem too awful, but something niggled at me. "Although, if it was Ghislain, why was he killed?"

Thor grunted.

I was not in the mood for conjecture with someone who wasn't using his words. I closed my eyes again, but a thought, just at the edge of my brain, still niggled. "We're missing something."

Thor grunted again.

I crossed my arms over my aching ribcage. I'd figure out what was bothering me when I didn't feel as if I'd been flattened by a steamroller. "Either one of them could have tipped off Diaz's people."

"What about your other friends?"

"Mia and André? No way."

I waited for a grunt, but it didn't come. Instead, Thor looked over his shoulder at me. His brow was wrinkled, and his chin was tucked. He looked almost as if he pitied me.

"It wasn't them." My voice was loud enough to catch the driver's attention. He looked at me in the rearview mirror with jaded eyes.

"Right." Thor shrugged.

Suppressing the urge to lean forward and smack him in the head was the hardest thing I'd done all night. I slipped my hands under my thighs.

"Can you tell me anything about the guy who saved us?" Thor asked. "Did you get a look at him?"

"You saw him. He was wearing a motorcycle helmet."

Another grunt. No surprise.

The drive to Neuilly went by too quickly. All too soon, Thor opened the back door and extended his hand to me.

I stood without his help. "You've got to be hurting as much as I am."

"I'm fine." He didn't look fine. Dark circles shadowed the skin beneath his eyes and his usually fluid movements were as jerky as a windup toy's.

I pushed myself clear of the car and together we lurched into the safe house.

Mr. Brown waited for us in his usual chair. "What the hell happened?"

We told him—the drugs in the wine, the intruders, the rappelling, the shooting, the guardian angel—everything.

"But you did as we asked, you went to the site on Lambert's computer?" Mr. Brown's brows were drawn and his lips tight.

Hadn't he been listening? "Yes, but what good will it do if Ghislain's dead?"

"Someone used his laptop."

"What site, sir?" Thor sounded properly respectful.

"Galeries Lafayette," replied Mr. Brown.

The men's gazes settled on me.

Seriously? "It wasn't me."

Neither Thor nor Mr. Brown looked convinced.

"Look—" I wiped my suddenly damp palms on my pants "—I did exactly as you asked, then I heard Thor running up the stairs."

"Thor?"

"Mark." The flush of heat on my cheeks wasn't exactly welcome. I ignored the warmth and kept talking. "I didn't have time to shop. And, if I did, it wouldn't be on Galeries Lafayette's website."

Mr. Brown raised a single brow.

"I'm in Paris. If I want to go shopping at Galeries Lafayette, I'll go to the actual store." There was logic no one could argue.

"Then who visited the site?"

"It must have been one of the men who broke into the apartment."

The way Mr. Brown pursed his lips let me know what he thought of that theory. "Who's the guy on the motorcycle?"

"No idea. I thought he worked for you."

"No. It seems someone wants you alive."

"Shouldn't that be you?"

Annoyance fluttered across Mr. Brown's forgettable face. "You knew the risks, Ms. Fields."

"There's more going on here than just Javier Diaz wanting me dead or Badawi wanting to know happened to his nephew."

Mr. Brown leaned forward and rested his forearms on his knees. "What makes you say that?"

"First off, there's the number of men sent to make sure I never walked out of Ghislain's apartment. Someone sent an army."

"And?"

"Aren't assassins supposed to be stealthy?"

"Not necessarily."

"The sheer number of killers seemed like someone was making a statement."

"What do you mean?"

"How many men does it take to kill one woman?"

"You have proven yourself to be remarkably resilient." Mr. Brown's voice was dry. Who would have guessed he had a sense of humor?

Not me. I bared my teeth at him.

Thor's grunt sounded almost like a laugh.

The thought that had been niggling at me wandered onto center stage in my brain and waved at the audience. "What if I wasn't the target?"

Both men regarded me with blank stares.

"Seriously," I insisted. "What if someone wanted Ghislain dead?"

"Why would someone want Lambert dead?" asked Mr. Brown.

"Someone has been after him to transfer money. Maybe they killed him after the transfers were complete."

"But why?"

"No idea."

"And who?" Mr. Brown looked down his nondescript nose.

"Someone who can put together an army. Have any of the dead men been identified?"

Mr. Brown's bland face grew serious. "One so far."

"Who was he?"

"Saif Rahim."

"Who?"

"A terrorist," explained Thor.

"That list of landmarks—"

Mr. Brown's serious expression darkened. "What list?"

I pulled up the picture of Ghislain's document and handed the phone to Mr. Brown. Had I stumbled onto a terrorist plot? "The Eiffel Tower's on there. And Gare du Nord. Plus the other locations Ghislain mentioned at the party."

Mr. Brown stared at the image for a moment, then gave the phone back to me. "We've had no inkling that Lambert does business with terrorists. He laundered money for drug dealers."

"Maybe he branched out." It was a reasonable suggestion.

Mr. Brown's gaze settled on me. "Do you really think a Frenchman like Lambert would be planning attacks on iconic sites in Paris?"

"No," I admitted.

"Maybe Lambert was planning a scavenger hunt."

That was the dumbest thing I'd ever heard. I glanced at Thor, but his face was unreadable.

"Our intel says you were the target." Mr. Brown took a sip of coffee. "Perhaps Diaz didn't appreciate his banker having dinner with a woman he wants dead. You've already cost him hundreds of millions of dollars."

Maybe Mr. Brown was right. Maybe Diaz's plan was to kill both of us. If so, you'd think the killers would come from Latin America, not the Middle East.

A man whose appearance was nearly as bland as Mr. Brown's appeared in the doorway to the salon. "I apologize for interrupting, sir, but there's a call you need to take."

"Who is it?"

"The director of SDAT, sir."

Mr. Brown shot Thor and me a look that could best be called *black*. Apparently getting calls from the French authorities wasn't on his to-do list for Paris. With a sigh, he stood. "I'll be back."

Thor and I were alone and I felt marginally better than I had in the car. I turned in my chair and scowled at him. "What were you thinking?"

"When?" The man looked mystified.

"When you went all heroic and chose not to run for that building."

He cocked his head to the side as if I'd presented him with a trick question requiring careful thought. "I was thinking I could save your life."

"You do realize you're my colleague and not my actual bodyguard, right?"

Thor grunted.

I looked at the ceiling and begged some higher power for patience. "I'm not helpless."

"I know that." He rubbed his eyes. "You're also not trained."

I clenched my hands into fists. "Doesn't matter."

"Does, too."

My nails cut crescents into my palms. "Does not."

We were one breath away from nanny-nanny-boo-boo.

I drew air deep into my lungs. "You are the second most annoying man I've ever met."

A wry smile twisted his lips. "Only the second?"

Jake was the first and Thor was nowhere near as annoying as Jake.

"Do you have any idea how much I dislike being thought of as a damsel in distress? I wasn't raised that way."

Thor raised a brow. He'd met Chariss. If ever there was a woman to raise a damsel daughter…

"I meant my father."

"Your father?"

"Before he died, he made sure I could protect myself."

Thor stretched out his legs and leaned his head back. "Listen, I know you're cranky, but shouldn't you save this lecture for the man who actually saved you?"

Cranky? That called for another deep breath. "He saved you, too."

Thor closed his eyes and his lips pinched together. "I know that."

I stared at the man in the chair. He looked exhausted. He sounded exhausted. He needed a break. Besides, I didn't have the energy for the complete scolding he so richly deserved. "Could we go back to the hotel? Please? I'm about to drop."

Thor opened one eye.

Mr. Brown strode back into the salon wearing his best sour-pickles expression. "The National Police want to talk to you."

"Oh, joy."

Thor snorted.

"Tell them they can come to the Ritz."

"You really want someone from the National Police in your suite?" asked Mr. Brown.

I sure as heck didn't want to wait for them in the safe house. "Yes."

"I'll have a driver take you and Stone back to the hotel."

"Thank you."

Mr. Brown turned his attention to Thor. "You said Lambert was dead."

Thor sat up and opened his second eye. "We heard a shot."

"His body wasn't in the apartment."

"What?" I stared at Mr. Brown.

"No body." Mr. Brown shrugged. "Maybe it was Lambert who was online shopping after you left."

Because that's what people did when their homes were invaded and World War III broke out in their car parks. I sealed my lips, keeping the sarcasm bubbling within me locked inside.

Mr. Brown's eyes narrowed. "You look tired."

"I am."

"The men from the National Police will come to your hotel."

Thor and I rode back to the Ritz in exhausted silence.

My thoughts made up for the lack of words. What happened to Ghislain? What was up with that lists of sites? Who had sent the posse of killers? Who'd saved us?

Plenty of questions. Not a single answer.

Two men stood as Thor and I entered the lobby.

"*Je suis LeBeau. Il est DuPont,*" said the shorter of the two.

They both pulled out badges. Not that they needed them. Even to my untrained eye, they looked like law enforcement. Men who'd had their senses of humor surgically removed.

Thor, who was looking fairly thunderous, took down their badge numbers and made a call. He listened for a moment, nodded, rattled off the badge numbers, and nodded again.

"This way." No inflection hinted at how little Thor wanted to talk to the National Police, but I heard it in his voice. Or maybe I was projecting.

LeBeau and DuPont followed us to the suite.

When the door closed behind us, even before I sat down, LeBeau asked, "You saw Badawi?"

"Yes." If I was a good hostess, I'd offer them drinks. I didn't. Instead, I curled in my favorite corner of the couch and waved at the various seats. It was as close as they were coming to an invitation.

"You're sure it was him?" LeBeau insisted.

"Positive." I told him all that transpired in Sevran.

DuPont, who was seated on a fauteuil, leaned forward. "What happened tonight?"

Thor told them.

"And you have no idea who came to your rescue?"

"None," I replied. "I wish I did. What happened to Ghislain?"

"We're looking for Monsieur Lambert." Now DuPont leaned back in his chair. "There have been four attempts on your life since you came to Paris?"

Had it been that many? "I suppose so."

"And how long have you been here?"

"Three days."

We all thought about that for a minute.

"The National Police will assign you protection," said LeBeau.

"Mr. Stone is protecting me."

Le Beau shook his head as if Thor wasn't worth counting. "We will add a second man. Perhaps with two guards, we can catch whoever is trying to harm you."

Thor looked more thunderous than ever. "We don't nee—"

The door to Chariss's bedroom flew open. "What in the hell is going on out here? I have an early ca—" She got a good look at me and Thor.

"Chariss, meet Monsieurs LeBeau and DuPoint. Gentlemen, this is my mother, Chariss Carlton."

The men from the National Police gaped at her.

"The actress?" LeBeau stood and extended his hand.

DuPont was right behind him.

"What happened tonight, Poppy? Are you all right?"

"Fine."

"There was an attempt on Miss Fields's life this evening." LeBeau wasn't helping.

"I see." You'd think trained agents would have heard the dangerous edge in Chariss's voice. "What happened?"

No one replied.

Chariss clutched the doorframe. "You're running out of lives."

"I hope not."

She shifted her attention back to LeBeau and DuPont. "You both look official. Which agency are you with?"

"The National Police."

"I see." Her eyes narrowed. "What exactly happened tonight?"

"We're still not sure," said LeBeau.

Chariss shifted her gaze my way. "Were you involved in that gun battle I saw on the news?"

"Yes."

Now she turned to Thor. "You're supposed to be protecting her."

"He did." I hated to bring her attention back to me, but she really couldn't blame Thor for the night's adventures.

"Pfft."

"I'm still alive. Tho—Mark did his job."

Now Chariss turned to the men from the National Police. "It's late. I'm sure any questions you have for my daughter will keep until the morning."

"Of course, Madame Carlton," said LeBeau.

Thor and I exchanged a look. Who knew it was so easy to get rid of the French policemen?

Not that I was complaining. I was too wiped out to do much more than nod from my spot on the couch. "Good night, messieurs." Yes, the National Police would send someone in the morning, but tonight I was too tired to care.

As soon as the door closed behind the Frenchmen, Chariss turned on me. "Are you trying to get yourself killed?"

"No."

She gave me a long, simmering look. "Well, it sure as hell looks that way to me."

SEVENTEEN

I slept like the dead. Deep. No dreams (which was probably a blessing). Waking up was like climbing an impossibly long, ridiculously steep set of stairs. I wanted to stay asleep. Wanted to close my eyes on death and guardian angels and the need for bodyguards.

But men's voices and annoyed yips assaulted my ears.

I dragged myself to the top of the I-don't-wanna-wake-up stairs, opened my eyes, and reached for my cell.

I lifted my head from the pillow and squinted. Seven in the morning? Ugh.

Gray light filtered through the window and I considered pulling the duvet over my head.

"*Yip.*"

Whatever was happening in the living room, Consuela had an opinion.

With a long-suffering sigh, I swung my legs over the edge of the bed, stood, and stumbled into the bathroom. The mirror was not my friend. Bruises marked my elbows and my knees. Shadowy half-moons darkened the skin beneath my eyes.

I ached, and not in a I-worked-out-so-hard-I-can-eat-all-the-carbs-I-want way. This ache was in my bones.

I mustered the energy to squeeze the toothpaste tube, brushed my teeth, and washed my face. When I poked at my hair, it poked back. I'd deal with the tangles later. After I'd had coffee. Lots of coffee.

I pulled on one the Ritz's bathrobes and opened the door to the main salon.

Thor and a man I didn't know sat on the couch. On the table in front of them, a basket of croissants, a pot of coffee, and an empty cup waited for me.

"You're up." Thor stood.

"Sort of." I had eyes only for the coffee.

"Monsieur Stone was telling me about your evening." The stranger stood, distracting me from my goal. He had to be in his forties. His hair was receding, stubble already darkened his lean cheeks, and his brown eyes were ancient. He had the air of a man who got things done. Difficult things. Things no one else could do. Chariss was going to love him. "I'm Jean Fortier."

"From the National Police?" I asked.

"Yes. I've been assigned to protect you."

I pulled the collar of the bathrobe tighter around my neck and sank into a chair. I hadn't expected anyone so early.

Consuela jumped off the couch and leapt into my lap.

"Coffee?" asked Thor.

"Please." I kissed the top of Consuela's head (kissing Thor would be inappropriate). "Is Chariss still here?"

"No. She left you a note." He handed me a folded piece of paper. I opened it and read, *Poppy, your cavalier disregard for your safety had me up all night. I know you're trying to prove you're more like your father than me—my therapist helped me see that—but I need my sleep. And what's wrong with being like me? I simply cannot make a movie and worry about you at the same time.*

I've spoken with the concierge and the hotel will be moving you to other accommodations.

Chariss had to be truly pissed off to kick me out. I stared at the paper in my fingers for a long moment, then crumpled it into a little ball. "Did you meet my mother, Monsieur Fortier?"

"No. I have not had the pleasure." He rubbed his chin and gazed at me with eyes that had seen too much. "Please, call me Jean."

I nodded and gratefully accepted the cup Thor was holding out to me.

Tap, tap.

Thor cracked the door to the suite and my best friend burst through it. "I just saw the news. Why didn't you call me? What the hell happened?"

I tightened my grip on the saucer. "I'm mentioned? On the news?"

"No. But I knew where you were going last night and the —" she searched for a word "—carnage is unbelievable." She planted her hands on her hips. "You're lucky to be alive."

"I know."

"You should go home to California. Today."

"Changing where I am wouldn't help."

"It wouldn't hurt either." She noticed Jean and held out her hand. "I'm Mia, Poppy's best friend."

"Jean Fortier." He gave no explanation for his presence.

They took each other's measure. An older man with world-weary eyes and a girl channeling Stevie Nicks.

Mia looked away first—looked at me. "What are you doing today?"

Everyone looked at me. Waiting.

"I'm going to Les Deux Magots for breakfast."

Thor's eyes narrowed. I'd picked a place on Lambert's list.

MIA'S LEFT BROW ROSE, her eyes widened, and a tic on her jawline suggested she was working to keep her jaw from dropping "Why would you do that?"

Thor nodded as if he seconded her question.

"Why wouldn't I?"

"Someone wants you dead."

"Last night probably threw a wrench in their plans." There had to be a finite number of assassins in Paris. Right? "Besides, I've never been."

"Only tourists go to Les Deux Magots."

"Just think, Simone de Beauvoir and Sartre drank there. And Hemingway."

Mia yawned.

"And Camus, Picasso, and James Joyce."

"Who?"

"James Joyce."

"Like a dead Irish guy is an incentive."

"You don't have to come." Life would be easier and she would be safer if she didn't. "But I've never been and I'm going."

Mia glanced at Thor and Jean (her gaze lingered on Jean). "Of course I'm going."

I drained my coffee cup and reached for the pot. I needed at least two cups before I dealt with my hair.

LES DEUX MAGOTS, named after two chinoiserie figurines, was across the street from Saint Germain des Prés. Tables on the sidewalk clustered under green awnings. Waiters with white aprons, black jackets, and slight sneers took coffee orders.

We took a table on the sidewalk and watched people on Boulevard St. Germain hurry past.

To our left, a table of Spaniards talked and sipped coffee.

To our right, an English couple perused the *Herald Tribune*. Marcel Charbeau was on the cover.

What was it about this place that landed it on Ghislain's list? I closed my eyes and imagined him sitting under the green awning. Imaginary Ghislain sneered at the foreigners.

"Poppy!"

"What?" I focused on Mia.

"I said your name three times."

"Sorry. I was thinking about something else." And I was tired. And achy. And worried.

"Obviously."

I offered her an apologetic smile.

"What are we doing after this?" We hadn't ordered yet and Mia already wanted to leave.

"Why?"

"I think there's a Bon Marché near here. I've never been."

The men looked at us with small, slightly superior smirks on their lips.

"You want to go shopping?"

"We are in Paris."

It was hard to argue that point. "Can't we just enjoy the moment?"

She snorted and waved over a waiter. "A double espresso."

"Café crème, please."

Thor and Jean ordered regular coffees.

My gaze wandered back to the sidewalk, where it landed on a short man with dark hair. My heart stuttered. Was it him? I tapped the back of Thor's hand. "That's one of them."

"What?" Thor turned his head from side to side. "One of who?"

"There." I jerked my chin toward the sidewalk. "Right there. He's one of the men from Sevran."

Thor stared at the man, who stood only feet away from us. "You're sure?"

"Positive."

Jean followed our gazes.

"Who are we staring at?" Mia demanded. "Do you see someone famous?"

The weight of our four stares settled on the man from Sevran's shoulders and he turned and looked at us—at me. His jaw dropped.

Thor jumped up from the table.

Jean grabbed his arm. "Stay with her." He meant me. Stay with me. But I couldn't argue the point because Jean was already lunging toward the short man.

And the short man was running.

Jean ran after him.

"What just happened?" Mia looked crestfallen.

Thor scanned the streets around us. "Poppy just spotted one of the men who tried to kill her." As awful as that sounded, it was still better than *Poppy just spotted an international terrorist who's been making suicide vests and stock-piling weapons*.

"Did he follow you here?" Now Mia was scanning the streets too. "Was he going to shoot at you or something?"

"I don't think so."

"He had to have followed us." Thor sounded so certain. "It's too big of a coincidence."

Maybe he was right. And if he was, sitting at a sidewalk café wasn't exactly smart. But maybe the man had been casing Les Deux Magots.

The waiter arrived with our coffees and Mia kicked back her espresso as if it was a shot of whiskey. "We should get out of here."

With a hand that barely shook, I lifted my coffee to my lips. "We can't leave without Jean." I was tired of running. And, if the terrorist had followed me, maybe the guardian angel had too. I scanned the sidewalk.

Was anyone watching us?

If they were, they were being very subtle.

"What now?" Mia demanded.

"We wait for a few minutes. If Jean doesn't return, we get in a cab and go back to the hotel."

I shook my head. "No."

Mia frowned at me. "No?"

"We go to Sacré-Couer."

A furrow appeared between her brows. "Why would we go there?"

"I've never been."

"You already used that reason once today."

"I didn't realize there's a limit. Beside, Les Deux Magots wasn't so bad. You enjoyed your coffee."

"I burned my throat. Jean just took off after someone who wants you dead. And it will take us an hour to get there."

"Do you have someplace you need to be?" Honey dripped off the end of my question.

"No. But we could go shopping or—" Mia struggled for something to do on a gray Paris morning other than shop "—or we could go to the Louvre."

"You? The Louvre?"

"I like art."

"Since when?"

"There's Jean." Thor cut through our spat.

Thor was right. Jean was walking toward us. Alone. His phone was pressed against his cheek and the expression on his face was grim.

He reached the table, sat, and downed his coffee in one bitter gulp. "He got away."

I'd figured that.

"There was a car waiting for him a few blocks down." Jean leaned toward me. "You're sure you saw that man with Badawi?"

"Yes."

His ancient eyes aged another twenty years or so. "*Putain.*"

Thor threw a hundred euros on the table. "We should go."

"To Sacré-Couer?" The rest of the table could go wherever they wanted. I was going to Montmartre.

"Why would we go to Sacré-Couer?" asked Jean.

"It's on the list."

"What list?" Jean and Mia spoke at the same time.

Jean didn't know about the list? I pulled up the picture of Ghislain's list on my phone and showed it to them.

Wrinkles creased Jean's brow. "You found this in Lambert's apartment?"

"Yes. Why?"

"I've seen a list of all documents pulled from his apartment and this paper was not included."

Who'd taken it? "I don't understand."

"I don't either." Jean rubbed his chin. "We looked into Lambert. He's a rabid nationalist. There's no way he'd help terrorists. Given half a chance, he'd wipe them from the face of France."

"Wait." Mia frowned at me. "The banker? That's the banker's list? You said he was just a banker."

"He was just a banker." A banker who laundered Mexican drug money and maybe helped terrorists.

"Was?" Her brows rose.

"He's dead."

"Maybe. Maybe not." Jean shrugged. "His body is missing."

I fiddled with the spoon that had come with my coffee. "Well, if he's not dead, it stands to reason he took the paper."

"The man was shot, and in all of his apartment, that piece of paper was the one thing he took with him?" Thor was a doubting Thomas.

I stared out at the throng on the sidewalk. "It doesn't

make any sense. But neither does him visiting the Galeries Lafayette website."

"How do you know that he did that?" Jean's voice was sharp.

Whoops. I looked down at my lap.

I felt the weight of Thor's thunderous glare.

I swallowed. Telling the National Police I'd planted what was probably an illegal tracker on a French citizen's computer might not be the smartest move.

"Don't answer." Jean held up his hand. "I don't want to know. Not now."

That was probably for the best. "So we're going to Sacré-Couer?"

"Wait." Mia held up her hands. "Shouldn't we tell the French authorities about all this?"

Thor, Jean, and I stared at her.

"Mia—" I spoke first "—Jean is the French authorities."

MIA WAS RIGHT. With the traffic, it took an inordinate amount of time to drive from the sixth arrondissement to Montmartre.

"How old is this church we're going to?" Mia could teach bored teenagers a thing or two about attitude.

"Not old," Jean replied. "Less than a hundred and fifty years."

"That's old."

"Not in Paris."

Mia stared out the window. "Then why is it famous?"

"Sacré-Couer was built as a sort of penance." Jean was wedged between Mia and me.

"Really?" I asked.

"French leaders vowed to build a church and dedicate it to

the Sacred Heart as reparation for France's sins." His shrug would probably have been more eloquent without Mia and me pressing against him. "People were a lot more religious then."

Some people still were. The man who'd just chased a terrorist should know that.

"What makes the building so white?" I asked.

"The travertine stone used to build the basilica exudes calcite when it gets wet and the stone turns white."

Mia yawned. "Are we even moving?"

We weren't. And when we did, our progress was measured in inches. "Should we walk?"

The taxi driver heard me. "I'm sorry it takes so long, mademoiselle. They are making a film and the delays in this part of the city are terrible."

"It's not your fault." I blamed Chariss. "We'll get out here."

We walked the next few blocks in silence. Thor and Jean were too busy scanning the crowd to talk and Mia was too annoyed with me to speak; her shoes were not made for walking.

"We can take the funiculaire to the top."

"We can take the what?" Mia asked.

"The funiculaire. It's like an elevator on the side of the hill —unless you want to climb two hundred steps." I was far too achy to climb all those stairs.

Mia looked down at her Blahniks. "Not likely."

We crammed into the funiculaire with what seemed like a hundred people—all of whom were snapping pictures on their phones.

Mia leaned forward and whispered in my ear, "I told you it would be like this. Nothing but tourists."

The ride lasted less than two minutes. At the top, we stepped out onto the Rue du Cardinal-Dubois. The damp air felt almost chilly. I buttoned my coat and stared at the chalky monument. Why had Sacré-Couer ended up on Ghislain's list?

A young boy jostled me and reflexively I tightened my grip on the handbag André had bought for me.

Jean grabbed the child's shoulder. "*Retourner le portefeuille de la jolie dame.*"

For an instant, the child looked as if he might argue, but something about Jean's eyes changed his mind.

He held out Mia's wallet.

She looked at the slim bit of leather and her jaw dropped. Without a word, she plucked her wallet from his hands.

Jean's grip on the boy's shoulder loosened and the child was gone, racing between clumps of tourists with practiced ease.

Mia blushed. She considered herself too worldly to be pickpocketed. "This place is nothing but a tourist trap."

"Or a holy site." Wry amusement curled Jean's lips into a grin. "It all depends on your perspective."

Mia blushed a deeper shade of rose. "Thank you for stopping him. I didn't realize he'd taken anything."

Jean shrugged. "The kids are good thieves."

I returned my gaze to the basilica. The only thing Sacré-Couer and Les Deux Magots had in common was the number of tourists milling around.

"I don't get it," said Thor, who stood next to me.

"I don't either."

"Let me see that list again," said Thor.

I pulled the photo up on my phone and handed it to him.

His brows drew together and I could almost see the wheels in his head turning. "Jean, how much do travel and tourism contribute to the French GDP?"

"About two hundred thirty billion."

"Billion?" The number was mind-boggling.

"*Oui.*"

"What if terrorists went after places tourists go?" Thor

pointed at the basilica. "Sacré-Couer, Les Deux Magots, the Eiffel Tower."

Jean rubbed at his chin. "It's possible, but Notre Dame is far more popular with tourists than Sacré-Couer. An attack there would strike at the heart of Paris. The cathedral is a better target."

"Maybe." I stared at a woman wearing ballet flats, pencil pants, and a stylish trench. She clutched at a cross hanging from her neck. "But you gave us a reason this place might be a target."

"I did?"

"You said Sacré-Couer was built as reparation for France's sins. There's symbolism in an attack here that there wouldn't be at Notre Dame."

Jean pulled his phone out of his pocket. "You really think there will be an attack?"

"I think it's possible."

Next to me, Thor nodded.

"I too think it's possible." Jean's finger hovered above a button on his phone. "May I take a picture of the list?"

Hadn't Mr. Brown already shared the list with someone at the National Police?

"I'll send it to you. What's your number?"

He gave me his number, waited until the photo showed up in his messages, and wandered a few paces away from us.

"You honestly think there's going to be a terrorist attack? Here?" Mia's pitch was higher than usual.

I watched Jean speak into his phone—his back was hunched, his shoulders stiff.

"You really think that?" Mia insisted.

"Maybe."

"Then why are we here?" she demanded.

"Because maybe we can stop it."

EIGHTEEN

"Have you lost your mind?" Mia's brows lowered and her eyes shot fire.

We knew the terrorists' targets. We knew the times of the attacks. All we were missing was the date. "We could make a difference."

"Poppy, be serious. What can you do?"

"Ouch."

"Keeping it real."

"I can recognize the men who were at the loading dock with Badawi."

"How many were there?" she asked.

"Two."

"Two guys—" she held up two fingers "— and how many targets? The chances you'd actually spot one of them have to be tiny." She pinched her fingers together. "That you recognized the guy this morning has to be some kind of miracle."

"So what do we do? Forget about it and go shopping?"

"We let him—" she pointed at Jean "—handle it."

"But—"

She held up her hands. "Can't you just let it go? It's not your problem. You're supposed to be on vacation. Vacation.

Fun. Shopping. Relaxation. Vacation's not supposed to mean danger or death or intrigue." She narrowed her eyes and glowered at Thor. "You're not saying much. You're the one who's supposed to keep her safe. Tell her to go back to the Ritz."

Thor shrugged. "She wants to make a difference."

"By getting herself killed?" Mia's pitch could shatter glass.

"Poppy is more resourceful than you give her credit for."

Mia pressed her hands against her temples. "I can't talk to you people."

"*Oui. D'accord.*" Jean's voice carried. He took the phone away from this ear, staring at it as if it was a pernicious weed.

"*Qu'est-ce qu'il passe?*" I asked. *What's happening?*

Jean's dark raincoat hung on his shoulders like a shroud. "There is a man at the National Police who wants to talk to you. He's sending a car."

I fished my phone out of my new handbag and looked at the screen. It wasn't yet eleven o'clock. There was still time. "Okay."

In deference to Mia's Blahniks, we rode the funiculaire down to the hill.

A white Renaut minivan with *Police Nationale* painted in blue on the hood waited for us near the merry-go-round at Place Saint-Pierre.

Mia raised her hand and waved at a taxi. "I'm catching a cab."

"Are you sure?" I hated it when Mia was mad at me. "You could come."

"I don't like police stations," she replied.

Neither did I. "Will you be all right?"

"Me? I'm going back to the Ritz and booking a massage, a facial, and a pedicure. I'll be much better off than you."

I hugged her. Steel beams were more pliable.

Finally, she softened. "Be careful. Please."

"I will."

Jean opened the door to the backseat and I climbed into the van. "Where are we going?"

"11 rue des Saussaies."

"Where?"

"Place Beauvau."

Place Beauvau I knew. I'd been to the Miu Miu store when it popped up. "Isn't that the Ministry of the Interior?" I hadn't noticed a building for the National Police.

"Yes."

"Why do they want to talk to me?"

"They don't. The National Police is housed in the Ministry's building. The inspecteur général of the judicial police has questions for you."

Thor and I exchanged a look. With one highly charged glance he told me I'd better not let slip that we'd done something to Ghislain's computer.

The drive from Montmartre was much faster with sirens. The van delivered us in front of the ministry and Jean ushered us inside.

We walked through a metal detector and a uniformed officer dug through my handbag.

He made Thor check his gun.

Jean led us to an office with an Aubusson on the floor, a baroque desk near the window, and Gen Paul paintings on the wall. "If you'll wait here, please. I'll be back in a few minutes." He disappeared down the hall.

I settled into a chair and whispered to Thor, "What has Mr. Brown told them?"

He shrugged. "I don't know."

"I realize he likes playing things close to the vest, but thi—"

"Bonjour, Mademoiselle Fields, Monsieur Stone." A man as elegant as the office paused in the doorway. "Thank you for speaking with us."

"My pleasure." I sized up the man who'd welcomed us.

Hair worn slightly too long. Beautifully cut suit. Charvet shirt. And—I narrowed my eyes—a Charvet tie. A man with means and taste, but there was something almost oily about him. He reminded me of Ghislain.

"Mademoiselle Fields, you have had an adventure since you arrived in Paris, yes?" He strolled into the office and propped himself on the edge of the desk.

"That's one way to describe it."

"Four attempts on your life, *n'est pas*?"

"Yes. I don't believe I caught your name."

"My apologies." He pressed his hand to his chest. "I am Phillipe Coligny. It is a pleasure to make your acquaintance. Would you care for coffee?"

"No, thank you." What time was it? The problem with depending on a cell for the time was the difficulty in sneaking a peek.

"I am told you talked to Ahmed Badawi."

"Yes."

"Here? In Paris?" His tone said he didn't believe me.

"Yes. We were in Sevran."

"This I find hard to believe."

"Oh?"

"For Badawi to come here, to Paris—" he wrung his hands "—it would be like Bin Laden visiting the United States after September eleventh."

"I saw him," I insisted. "I talked to him. He asked me about his nephew."

"His nephew?"

"His nephew was killed in a hacienda in Sinaloa, Mexico. Badawi wanted to know the circumstances of his death."

Phillipe's raised brows suggested only mild interest. "It would be too great a risk for him to come here."

"Why?"

"He would be caught."

"He was in Sevran."

"It's not possible. Someone would see him."

"Aren't there no-go zones in Sevran?"

A dark cloud passed over Phillipe's face. "An exaggeration."

Not from what I'd seen. "My point is that Badawi could easily hide in a neighborhood like that."

"We have technology, cameras—we would know if he was here." Phillipe turned to Thor. "Did you see Badawi?"

"No. But if Poppy says she talked with him, she did."

"It is possible Mademoiselle Fields is mistaken. She'd been abducted. She was afraid. She—"

"I saw him."

He shrugged. We were at an impasse.

"What about the list?" I asked.

Phillipe's gaze settled on me for an instant, then bounced away. He raked his fingers through his mane. "This idea—that an attack is imminent, that Ghislain Lambert might be involved—" he shook his head "—it's impossible. My father and his grandfather were friends. There is no way Lambert would be part of an attack on Paris."

I crossed my arms and leaned back in my chair.

He focused entirely on Thor. "Lambert was brought to your attention because there was an idea he might be laundering money." Phillipe flicked his fingers. "This was a false idea. I told your Mr. Brown, such a thing was impossible."

Ghislain had definitely been up to something. "Be that as it may—"

"*Non!*" He held up a single finger and wagged it at me. "Ghislain Lambert loved his country. He would never put France at risk."

There was no point in arguing with the man. "As you wish, monsieur."

"This list you saw. It cannot be a list of targets. The only chatter we have heard about an attack focuses on the Louvre. And, I assure you, we have extra security onsite."

This was Jean's boss? The man was a pompous ass with his head in the Seine.

My handbag vibrated. "Excuse me." I grabbed my cell. André was calling and the time was eleven thirty. "I'll just switch this off."

Phillipe pursed his lips.

"Sorry." I wasn't. Not really.

"As I was saying—"

Jean entered the office. His gaze traveled from Phillipe to me to Thor and his eyes narrowed.

I'd known the man less than five hours. I couldn't count on him to back me up.

"I was just telling Mademoiselle Fields there is no way Ahmed Badawi could be in France."

Jean raised a single brow. "Oh?"

"And it is not possible that Ghislain Lambert would support terrorists working in France."

Jean nodded his chin. Once. Ceding Phillipe's point.

"Mademoiselle Fields should return to her hotel." Phillipe shifted his gaze to Thor and winked. "You should take her to the Louis Vuitton store. It's just across the street from the Ritz."

I ground my molars together.

"Although—" he shrugged "—with all the Chinese so eager to get inside, I hear there are lines to buy a handbag."

It was official. The man was an idiot.

"We should consider all that Mademoiselle Fields has to say," said Jean.

"There is no way Badawi is in France." Phillipe Coligny wasn't just an idiot. He was a stubborn idiot. And an ass.

Jean rubbed his chin. "The attacks of November thirteenth, they were timed to spread our resources thin."

The upper corner of Phillipe's lip quivered as if a sneer was pushing at his mouth.

"Imagine major attacks all over the city."

"Attacks on Gare du Nord and Sacré-Couer and Le Tour Eiffel? They are too well guarded." Phillipe flicked his fingers again, dismissing the mere idea of coordinated attacks.

The landmarks might be well guarded, but the people around them weren't. We were wasting our time. I stood. "I have one request, Monsieur Coligny."

"What is that?"

"If Gare du Nord is attacked, you'll immediately send men to Pompidou."

The Frenchman rolled his eyes. "Do not worry, mademoiselle. We are very good at our jobs."

Not that I'd noticed, but arguing would be a waste of breath.

"We will send men and we will evacuate," said Jean. "You have my promise."

Phillipe pushed away from the edge of the desk. "But, sir—"

Sir?

"Go. Have the terrorism alert moved to the highest level."

Phillipe blinked.

I did, too.

Jean slid behind the elegant desk and sat. "There has been an attack in Marseilles and my superior, the inspector general, has left for the south of France. It was an emergency and he apologizes for bringing you here and leaving before your arrival. He very much wanted to talk to you. I assure you, we are taking the threats you discovered seriously." He turned to Phillipe. "Coffee for Mademoiselle Fields."

"She doesn't want any."

"Get it anyway."

With that, Phillipe Coligny departed.

"I'm sorry your trip here is wasted, and I apologize for Phillipe."

"You are..." Thor sounded stunned.

"The director of SDAT."

What did that mean? "SDAT?"

"*Sous-direction anti-terroriste.*"

"And you just decided to spend the morning with us?"

Jean pressed his hands together, then tapped them against his chin. "Your Mr. Brown told us you'd talked to Badawi. I wanted to see if you were credible."

"Am I?"

"Very."

"What can I do?"

"Nothing. We are on highest alert. Thank you for your time, Miss Fields."

I'd been dismissed. I shifted in my seat.

"I'll have a car take you to the Ritz."

"That's all right."

"I insist." He wanted me safely out of the way.

"I saw the Fendi pop-up when we pulled up. I'd rather go there."

He leveled a disbelieving gaze my way. "I see. Stay away from Gare du Nord, Miss Fields."

"Of course." Gare du Nord was far too big for me to spot a terrorist. I had a much better chance at Les Halles and Pompidou.

Thor escorted me out of the office, down a sweeping flight of stairs, and out the ornate front gates into Place Beauvau.

I walked toward the Fendi store.

"You seriously want to go shopping?"

"No, but that's what I told Jean we were doing." I led him toward the boutique. "This space has already been both a Prada and Miu Miu pop-up."

"Pop-up?"

"A limited-time-only store. Here for a few months, then gone." We pushed through the glass door, I picked up the nearest handbag, and looked into his eyes. "What are we going to do?" I meant about the terrorist attacks, not the shopping. I knew what to do about the shopping.

"There's not much we can do."

He was right. I sighed and took in the shop's zebra wood walls, the glass shelves holding beautiful bags, and the gold mannequins wearing the latest in prêt-à-porter. "I want a gun."

Thor's jaw dropped. "You what?"

I put the bag back on the shelf. "I want a gun."

"Why?"

"Because I have a feeling I'm going to need it."

Thor merely stared at me.

I let him stare and fingered the sleeve of a floral trench. "I think I'll try this on. Here—" I shoved my handbag into his hands and slipped my arms into the coat's sleeves "—what do you think?"

He grunted.

"I think it's fabulous."

"So you'll take the coat and a gun."

"And that handbag." I caught a saleswoman's eye and pointed to a Peekaboo in a soft shade of pink.

She hurried toward us—well, hurried as much as a terminally chic Frenchwoman forced to wait on an American ever could.

"*Ce sac à main et cette tranchée florale.*" I pointed toward the coat.

"*Puis-je vous aider avec autre chose?*"

No. I'd bought quite enough. "*Non, merci.*" I handed her my American Express card and turned back to Thor. "Where do I get a gun?"

He pinched the bridge of his nose and shook his head. "We'll have to go to Neuilly."

"Fine."

"You're serious about this?"

"Jean seems like a decent guy. I think he'll do all he can to stop whatever's happening, but I have a terrible feeling I'm going to need a gun."

"You don't even know what day whatever's happening will happen."

"True," I ceded. "But I want to be prepared and—"

"And?"

I had a sinking feeling that whatever was happening would happen soon. "And I need a gun."

Thor grunted. "Fine."

"That was easy." I'd expected more of an argument.

"You know that terrible feeling you have?"

Too well. I nodded.

"I have the same one."

We took the Metro to Neuilly and walked the few blocks to the safehouse.

Thor led me to an armory and presented me with a Glock.

"What now?" he asked.

I glanced at my phone. It was well past noon. "Back to the city? Can you get a car?"

"First a gun, now a car. What next?"

"What are you doing here?" Jake stood in the door to the armory and he didn't look happy to see me.

"Picking something up." Vague was good.

"What?" he demanded.

Thor rubbed the back of his neck. "A Glock."

Jake's eyes widened and his lips narrowed. "For Poppy? Are you insane?"

"I'm a very good shot." I was. My father had taught me.

"You can't carry a gun in France. It's against the law." That was rich coming from Jake.

"Since when do you care about breaking the law?"

He opened his mouth, but no words came out.

"If I'm right about these attacks, my having a gun will be the least of the French authorities' worries."

"The attacks?"

"The attacks Badawi has planned." Had Mr. Brown not told him?

"What attacks?"

The phone in my handbag buzzed. I thrust my hand into the depths and pulled out my cell. I held up my finger, putting Jake off. "What?"

"Are you all right?" André sounded genuinely concerned.

"I'm fine. Sorry I barked at you."

"I'm worried. Mia said you were chasing terrorists."

"That's the National Police's job."

"So you're not doing something incredibly dangerous? Promise?" He sounded doubtful. "Where are you now?"

"I've been shopping at the Fendi pop-up." Not exactly a lie, but not the whole truth. "I bought a trench and a Peek-aboo bag."

"Another bag?"

"The one you bought me will always be my favorite."

Thor and Jake were watching me with slightly stunned looks on their handsome faces.

"What are you doing?" I asked.

"I have a meeting with your mother."

"With Chariss? Why?"

"There's a promotion opportunity. I'm going to meet her at her shoot. She's in Montmartre this afternoon. At Sacré-Couer."

That was wrong. I'd seen her calendar. "Chariss is at the Moulin Rouge today."

"They changed the schedule."

My stomach free-fell through the floor. "André, don't go to Montmartre. Don't go anywhere near Sacré-Couer. Promise me."

"What? Why?"

"Just promise me!"

"Okay, fine. I promise. What's go—"

"I've gotta go. I have to call Chariss. Bye." I hung up the phone and dialed my mother.

The call went to voicemail. She was probably ignoring my calls.

"Chariss, get away from Sacré-Couer. Please, for me, just do it." I ended the call and looked up at Thor and Jake.

They were both staring at their phones with matching expressions of horror on their faces.

"What? What happened?"

"There's been an explosion at Gare de Nord."

NINETEEN

"We have to go. Now." My fingers flew over the keyboard on my cell. If Chariss wouldn't take my calls, maybe she'd read my text. Please, God, let her read my text. UR in danger. GET AWAY from Sacre-Couer. I thought for a moment and added, PLEASE.

Meanwhile, Thor opened drawers and pulled out clips of ammunition. "We're going to Sacré-Couer?"

"You can't go there." Jake's face was a study in stubborn.

"What do you mean I can't?" Who made him boss? "Of course I can. I have to."

Jake crossed his arms and blocked the doorway to the hall. "Fortier will have this handled."

"Fortier will have his hands full. There's just been an explosion at the busiest train station in Europe. Thirty minutes from now something awful will happen at Pompidou. And, even if he didn't have two catastrophes to deal with, he wouldn't look out for Chariss." I glanced at my phone again. "We don't have much time." An hour. We had an hour.

"There are people all over Paris who deserved to be

saved." Jake's voice was too calm, too reasoned—it set my teeth on edge.

"I'm not arguing your point." I totally was. "But she's my mother."

"You don't even like your mother."

That stopped me—for about five seconds. "That might be true. But I do love her. Besides, things have been better lately. There's no way Chariss and I can fix our relationship if she's dead." I slipped the Glock and the clips Thor held out to me into my handbag. "Are you coming?"

"You can't do this!"

"Dammit, Jake." Did he really think me so incapable? "You can't talk me out of this. So, are you coming or not?"

"This is insane. Do you even have a plan?"

"The plan is to save my mother. Are you coming?"

Jake pressed his fingertips to his forehead as if I'd asked a difficult question like how algebra worked or the meaning of life. He shifted his gaze to Thor. "You're going along with this?"

"What would you do if it was your mother?"

Jake scowled. "I should have known you'd be on board with whatever she wanted."

What was that supposed to mean?

Jake's face darkened. "She's got you wrapped so tightly around her finger, you can barely breathe."

Thor simply stared. "You can't keep treating her like a porcelain doll. She took out a terrorist with a pen. She's tough enough to handle an op."

"She got lucky."

"I'm standing right here." My speaking reminded Jake he was scowling at the wrong person.

He turned his scowl my way. "You could be killed."

"Chariss could be killed."

Jake, whose face had turned a deep shade of red, shifted his scowl back to Thor. "Could you give us a minute?"

Thor looked at me and raised a single brow.

I answered him with a small nod.

Jake stepped away from the entrance, allowing Thor to leave. "You can't do this. I can't do this."

"Do what?"

"Watch you throw yourself in harm's way. You're not cut out for this."

Every second Jake spent telling me how I wasn't capable of making a difference or saving my mother was a second off the clock.

"You know how I feel about you," he continued. "I need you to be safe." He reached out his hand as if he meant to brush his fingers against my cheek.

I stepped backward.

This wasn't about his feelings. It was about Chariss.

I raised my index finger and poked him in the chest. Hard. "Either you believe in me, or you don't. Either way, I have to go. Now." I pushed past him.

"Please, Poppy." His voice was filled with pain. "Don't."

I stopped. I even turned. "Has it occurred to you we could stop whatever Badawi has planned at Sacré-Couer?"

"The National Police should handle this. It's their problem. Not ours."

"Maybe not yours," I ceded. "But my mother is there. It is totally my problem." I left him standing in the doorway.

Thor waited for me outside the front door. He'd commandeered a Peugeot.

I climbed into the passenger seat.

"Jake's not coming?"

My shoulders tightened. "I guess not. Let's go."

We were on Avenue Charles de Gaulle in less than a minute. Thor wove expertly through traffic as we raced back to the city. "What's the fastest way to Montmartre?"

"The Boulevard Périphérique." The parkway that circled Paris would definitely be the fastest route.

"Got it. Would you check your phone? See if there are any updates?"

I opened Twitter. "They're saying it was a train that exploded." I scrolled. "And authorities aren't letting anyone onto the Périph. We'll have to cut through the city."

"Got it." He raced past the access road and sped toward the Arc de Triomphe.

Only the bravest foreigners will attempt a drive around the star at the Arc de Triomphe. Cars merged and honked and switched lanes without a passing thought to other motorists.

That we ended up on Avenue de Wagram without a collision counted as a win. That we were actually headed north counted as a miracle.

"After that, terrorists should be easy." Thor's fingers were clenched around the steering wheel in a death grip and there was a tic near his eye. "Where do I go from here?"

I pulled up directions on my phone. "Take a right up ahead." We turned onto Boulevard des Batignolles.

He glanced at me. "Your leaning forward won't make the car go any faster."

"Sorry." I sat back. "We don't have much time."

"Where do I go next?"

I pointed. "Get on Boulevard de Clichy."

The closer we got to Montmartre, the more congested the streets became. I rolled down the window. "Do you hear any sirens?"

"No. Why?"

"If they were evacuating around Sacré-Couer, we'd hear sirens."

"What time is it?"

I looked at my cell. "1:35."

"Check on Pompidou."

I opened Twitter and read. The phone slipped through my fingers and fell to my lap.

"What?"

I crossed my arms over my stomach. "Multiple shooters have opened fire. The attack is happening now."

Thor's jaw firmed and he punched the gas pedal. "Someone is tweeting about it live?"

"He's telling his family he loves them." My eyes filled with tears and my hands fumbled for my phone. In thirty minutes, something terrible would happen at Les Deux Magots. In less than an hour, terror would visit Sacré-Couer.

The roads were filling up as frightened Parisians took to the streets. Thor was forced to turn multiple times just to keep us moving forward. Finally, the streets became so congested he pulled over. "It would be faster on foot."

"Fine." My hand was already on the door handle.

To our right was Le Clos Montmartre, Paris's only vineyard.

"Road's closed." Thor pointed to an armed gendarme. Rue des Saules was not an option.

At least the policeman's presence was a hopeful sign.

I grabbed Thor's arm and pulled. We ran up Rue Saint-Vincent. "We can cut through here."

Narrow steps were cut between the vineyard and the Jardin Sauvage.

"Where are we?" asked Thor as the foliage from a horse chestnut trees whapped him in the face.

"That's the Jardin Sauvage. It was a fallow field until nature reclaimed it. Paris made it a park. We're coming up behind the Musée Montmartre."

"How do you know all this?"

"I know Paris."

"The Musée de what?"

"De Montmartre. Renoir used one of the houses as a studio. It's a museum now."

Thor muttered something about the number of museums in Paris. His voice was barely audible above the sound of gravel crunching beneath our shoes and the beating of my heart in my ears.

"What time is it?"

He glanced at his watch. "We're okay."

We had time. It was my new mantra. *We had time. We had time. We had time.*

But not much. I climbed faster. The stairs led to the museum's gardens. We skirted the first building, scurried across the lawn with its circular reflecting pool and artfully scattered patio furniture, dashed through the gate into a grassy courtyard, and emerged onto Rue Cortet.

The street was narrow and cobbled and eerily empty.

"That way." I pointed to the left. "We're almost there. We'll come out behind Sacré-Couer."

We ran through Montmartre's narrow cobbled streets, past a creperie with a red door, past stores selling cheap souvenirs —postcards, T-shirts, and squares of polyester pretending to be silk twill scarves. We flew past a near-empty bistro, a gallery selling appallingly bad art, and an Irish pub. And there it was. The back of Sacré-Couer.

Our heels rang against the cobblestones of Rue de Cardinal Guibert. *We still had time.*

A broad pedestrian plaza stretched in front of the basilica.

I slowed, caught my breath, scanned the crowded plaza. It shouldn't have been so easy to reach Sacré-Couer. Where were Jean Fortier's men?

There were cameras, cameramen, and Chariss's director, a nervous man who existed on coffee and cigarettes. He was raking his fingers through his hair and barking at his staff. There were tourists. There were extras. There was litter. Empty Evian bottles, plastic sacks, and cigarette butts. There was a group of schoolchildren holding hands. There were even a few police officers.

There was no Chariss.

I scanned the crowd more carefully.

"What time is it?"

"We have ten minutes."

There! There she was. How had I missed her? Her bright yellow rain slicker with green stripes was like a beacon. She stood at the top of the stairs, gazing out at Paris spread beneath her.

"Chariss!" I called.

She didn't respond. Didn't even move.

Perhaps she hadn't heard me. Perhaps the conversation she was having with the man standing next to her claimed all her attention.

I hurried toward them.

The man turned and glanced back at the basilica.

I froze. "It's one of them."

"Who?" Thor demanded.

"The guy who's standing next to Chariss. He was with Badawi in Sevran." I recognized his heavy brows, the crook of his nose, and the gap between his front teeth.

"He makes six."

"Six?"

"Six bad guys."

We could take six. "You're sure that's all?"

"Six I can see. There could be more."

"Why doesn't Jean have more police here?"

Thor looked down at the city below us and frowned. "He's keeping people away. If you had limited resources and knew the targets, which one would you try and save?"

"The Eiffel Tower." My answer was immediate. But what about all the people who were here at Sacré-Couer? They were minutes away from disaster. "We have to stop Badawi's men."

"How?"

I shrugged, at a loss. "I'm open to ideas."

"We take them out before they attack."

"How sure are you that there are only six? Where are they?"

"Dotted around."

"And you're positive the men you've spotted are bad guys?" I didn't want to shoot an innocent man.

Thor grimaced. "A hundred percent positive?"

"Yes."

"I'm sure about the guy with your mother and the guy at the gate to the steps of the basilica."

"You're only sure about two?"

"If you want one hundred percent positive, yes. The rest are just likely."

"Where are the other four?"

"Mixed in with the crowds." Thor glanced back at the basilica. "You take the guy by the gate. I'll save your mom."

"What? Why?" I should save Chariss.

"He'll recognize you."

Thor was right.

I exhaled.

"Go now." He pointed me toward the basilica.

"Fine." I turned.

"Poppy."

"What?"

"Be careful."

"You, too." There were a thousand words I could have added. Instead, I walked across the plaza.

I put on my best harmless-as-a-kitten expression, opened my handbag, and peered inside. Not that there was much inside. Wallet. Makeup bag. Gun.

With my head bent, I approached the man by the gate. Unlike the rest of the people milling around, all of whom wore light raincoats, he had on a parka.

Maybe that was why he was sweating.

As I watched, he unzipped his coat enough for me to catch sight of a vest. A suicide vest. The heavy parka hid death.

My feet tripped over a cobblestone and I barely kept myself from falling.

I could shoot him now—from a safe distance—but I might cause a panic and the other members of the six might trip the explosives on their vests.

Why hadn't Jean evacuated the site?

I gathered my courage and stumbled toward the man on the stairs, cutting off the teacher leading her students toward the basilica. "They're in danger," I whispered. "Get them out of here."

The teacher looked at me, her eyes wide.

"Take them to the Musée Montmartre. You should be safe there."

She didn't move.

"Gare du Nord has been attacked. And Pompidou. Sacré-Couer is next."

Her cheeks paled, but she turned to the children and said, "*Par ici.*" She led them past the entrance and toward the side of the basilica.

Now I just had to stop an attack. I bumbled my way to within a few feet of the gate. "*Excusez-moi, monsieur.*" I smiled up at the man.

He looked at me with young eyes. He couldn't be twenty years old and he was willing to die.

I was close enough to see the peach fuzz on his round cheeks. Close enough that if he detonated his vest I'd be vaporized. I widened my smile. "*Quelle heure est-il?*" *What time is it?*

He looked down at his watch.

Now or never. I swung my arm across my body, then cut my hand toward his head. The outer heel of my palm connected with his temple.

He collapsed.

I caught him and lowered him to the steps.

The man was out cold. I unzipped his coat and gazed at

the vest. I had no earthly clue how to defuse the thing. Quickly, I rezipped his coat, and looked over to the spot where Badawi's man had stood with Chariss.

Thor's body sprawled across the cobblestones.

A spike in adrenaline robbed my mouth of moisture and turned my hands to icicles.

I ran. The slick soles of my ballet flats sliding on the stones.

"Mark!" I fell to my knees next to him.

"Knife." His voice was faint.

That's when I saw a handle protruding from his gut.

"Don't take it out."

"I won't. Where's Chariss?"

He turned his head slightly and I followed his gaze.

Badawi's man had dragged Chariss down the stairs to the street below. He was pulling her toward a waiting car.

I reached into my purse and pulled out the Glock.

It had been too long since I'd been to a range. I couldn't shoot at him—I might hit Chariss.

But with each passing second, he pulled her closer to the car. I closed my eyes and imagined the televised beheading of an American movie star.

Bile rose in my throat.

I shifted my aim to the right and shot out one of the car's tires.

Somewhere near me a woman screamed.

I kept my gaze on Chariss. Right up until an explosion knocked me flat.

I lay on the damp cobblestones for a moment, almost afraid to move, to learn which parts of me wouldn't respond to my brain's signals.

I flexed my toes. I tightened my fingers around the gun. Surely fingers and toes working were a good sign. I pushed up onto my hands and knees and glanced back at Sacré-Couer.

One of Badawi's men had detonated his vest.

There were people on the cobblestones. People moaning. People screaming. People not moving.

I covered my mouth with my free hand.

"Poppy!"

I looked up at Jake.

"Are you hurt?" Jake's usually golden aura had turned crimson with rage.

"No." I shook my head. "How did you get here so fast?"

"I had Fortier let me onto the Périph."

"I didn't think you were coming."

"I'm sorry."

"There are more terrorists."

"We've got three. Someone knocked out the guy closest to the basilica."

"That was me."

He winced. "Figures."

"Mark is hurt."

"Ambulances are on their way."

"Is there a surgeon at the embassy?"

"Yes."

"Take him there."

"What? Where are you going?"

I shifted my gaze to the street below. "I'm going after Chariss."

TWENTY

The lawn stretching in front of Sacré-Couer filled with people running in fear.

I paused at the overlook on the Rue du Cardinal Dubois and searched the crowd. There they were! Chariss's yellow jacket was easy to spot.

Chariss was giving Badawi's man fits. She was digging in her heels and struggling and swinging her free arm at him.

Their progress was slow.

I hid my gun under the folds of my trench coat, dashed down the flight of steps to the lawn, and ran after them.

The earth beneath my feet was damp and the grass was slick. I skidded as I ran.

Boom!

I fell forward, landing on my knees.

Another explosion? I looked back at Sacré-Couer. The basilica was still standing, ghostly white in the falling mist. But what about Thor? What about Jake? Panicked screams and heartbreaking sobs tumbled down the hill. There were people hurt, dying.

My stomach churned

What should I do? Could I help? Should I return to the basilica?

I shifted my gaze to Chariss.

Badawi's man was also looking back at Sacré-Cœur, and he was grinning as if the explosion was a reason to celebrate, as if other people's pain brought him pleasure.

Chariss jerked away from him, almost breaking his hold on her arm. "*Au secours!*"

Badawi's man jerked her forward and she tripped. He yanked her back to her feet and her anguished cry reached me.

That cry decided me. I ran after them.

"*Au secours!*"

A guy in a windbreaker stopped in front of them. I couldn't hear what he said—he was too far away and the blood in my ears roared too loudly—but whatever it was, Badawi's man didn't like it.

He shot the poor guy between the eyes and pulled Chariss away before the body hit the ground.

The people near them scattered.

As for Chariss, seeing a man murdered in front of her seemed to drain all of her fight. She limped along, hardly bothering to dig in her heels.

Dammit. I needed her to fight.

"Chariss!"

My voice was lost amongst the screams still coming from the basilica, the sirens in the streets, and the cries of the people racing down the hill with me.

Chariss and Badawi's man slipped and slid on the wet grass.

I slipped and slid after them.

Where was he taking her? Was there another car waiting? Chariss and the terrorist were almost to the street.

"Chariss!"

She didn't even turn her head.

I ran. My breath came in short pants, and out of nowhere, a stitch lanced my side. I stumbled and fell on the wet grass. My ankle twisted beneath me.

There was no time for falling down. I hauled myself off the ground and took a step. Pain shot up my leg and I cried out.

That Chariss heard.

She dug in her heels and turned.

The expression on her face when she saw me would have been comical if our situation hadn't been so dire. Her mouth formed a perfect circle and her eyes widened to twice their normal size.

Badawi's man spotted me too. But his reaction was different.

The dark slashes of his brows drew together. He raised his gun.

I raised mine.

His eyes narrowed.

"Let her go."

The man holding Chariss had dead, soulless eyes, but something flickered in them when I spoke.

"Let her go," I repeated.

"Do you think a girl can affect our plans?" His voice was a sneer.

"Chariss wasn't part of your plan."

"She is a symbol of American rot." His eyes flickered again and this time I recognized the flame. Evil. Killing Chariss, a symbol of American rot, on the internet would be a feather in his terrorist cap. He might need a feather since Sacré-Couer was still standing.

Chariss whimpered.

Dammit.

Now would be a good time for her to channel some of the kickass heroine she was portraying in her new movie. Instead, she stood there drenched and silent and beaten.

Rain flattened my hair to my head and snuck past my collar, rolling down my back in cold trickles. "She's just an actress."

"She is dead." He lifted his gun an inch. "And so are you."

Chariss didn't respond. It was as if she were in shock. Her mascara traced black rivulets on her cheeks. Was it rain or tears that had melted her make-up? She was definitely crying. She looked nothing like the Chariss I knew. No glamour. No beauty. No sexiness.

Badawi's man lifted the gun another inch.

Chariss came alive. "You will not hurt my daughter." She kicked the man's junk hard enough to double him over.

Then she tugged free of his grasp, grabbed my wrist, and pulled me down the hill, past the merry-go-round, and into the street.

Pulling me wasn't easy. My twisted ankle slowed me down and a strange half-laugh, half-sob had taken hold of my lungs.

The street was chaos. Panicked tourists pushed their way into the café facing the grassy hill as if its glass windows might act as a barrier to bombs or guns. An accident snarled traffic and frightened drivers had abandoned their cars. Scared shop owners lowered the graffiti-marked steel doors that protected their stores from theft.

Chariss ran past all that. And she dragged me with her.

"Where are you going?" I gasped. The pain shooting through my ankle left me near breathless.

"Away from here." Chariss's eyes were wild.

"Wait." I pulled against her grip.

She slowed. "What?"

"My ankle." I glanced behind us. "That man will be following us."

"What?" Her eyes grew wider. "Why?"

"I don't know why. I just know he will. You should take off that coat."

She looked down at her yellow slicker. "It's from Stutterheim."

"Really? Is it worth getting shot over?"

She shrugged out of the coat and let it drop to the pavement. "Where do we go?"

"Up." I pointed to the two hundred steps that led up to Sacré-Couer and my leg throbbed with anticipatory pain.

"There are terrorists up there."

"There are even more police."

"And you think you can climb all those stairs?" She looked down at my already swelling ankle.

"I don't have much choice."

We climbed.

The stairs were empty. Those running away from Sacré Couer had already descended.

I would have liked more people, if only for camouflage. But we were alone. Each step was agony. And we were easy targets.

I anticipated a bullet in my back with each breath.

I took another step and gasped as pain shot all the way to my hip. Surely we were close to the top. I looked up. We hadn't yet reached the halfway point. "I can't."

"Don't be ridiculous." Chariss didn't let me stop. She wrapped her arm around my waist and willed me forward.

I made it up another fifteen steps before my ankle gave way and I tumbled to the stone. I couldn't take another step. Could not. "Go," I told her. "You can get help."

She looked at the steep expanse above us and a mulish expression settled on her face. "I'm not leaving you."

"Your getting help might mean that both of us make it through this alive."

"Are you crazy?" She planted her hands on her hips. "We should have hidden that raincoat. If he finds it, he'll know which way we've gone. He could be following us right now."

"I'll sit here with my gun and be ready to shoot him if I

see him." I twisted and sat so I faced the steps below us. Somehow we'd climbed at least a hundred.

"I can't just leave you."

"Yes, you can. If you hurry, you'll be able to get help before he finds me."

She didn't move.

"Go."

She looked down the stairs. No one was following us. Yet.

"Go."

She took a single step. "Poppy—"

"What?" She needed to go.

"I love you."

My throat tightened. "I love you too, Mom. Now, go."

She ran up the stairs with the ease of an actress who spent two hours a day with a personal trainer.

I wiped the rain—definitely rain—out of my eyes and returned my gaze to the bottom of the stairs. Would she return with help before Badawi's man found me?

There was no cover on the steps, no place to hide from a bullet.

The rain picked up. Fat, cold drops beat down on me so heavily I couldn't see the bottom of the stairs.

On the plus side, someone standing at the base looking up probably couldn't see me.

I rested my wrist on my knee. I was cold. I was wet. I was miserable. When I'd thought about making a difference I hadn't imagined anything like this. At least Sacré-Couer still stood. And those children—surely they'd made it to safety before the first bomber had detonated his vest. I straightened my shoulders and peered down the steps.

Was that movement?

I tightened my grip on the gun.

Bang!

Shards of stone bit into my cheek.

Badawi's man had found me. I was out of time.

I crouched as close to the steps as humanly possible and squinted into the gloom. Where was he?

"C'mon." A man in jeans and a black hoodie slid his arm around my torso and hauled me off the step. "Let's get you out of here."

Where had he come from? I stared up at him, unable to speak or move.

"C'mon." He spoke with American impatience.

"Did Chariss send you?"

He snorted.

"I can't walk."

"I'll carry you."

I glanced at the hundred steps rising above us. From what I could see in the rain, he was fit. But it would take The Rock to carry me to the top.

"Trust me." He swept my knees out from under me and held me in his arms.

I had no choice but to trust him.

"Keep an eye out for Sayed."

"For who?"

"Sayed Hamadei. The guy trying to kill you. If you see him, don't hesitate. Shoot."

He climbed the first step as if it were nothing to carry a grown woman in his arms.

"Sayed would rather kill me than escape?" It wasn't really a question. I already knew the answer.

"He can't stand to lose to a woman." He was climbing stairs as if I weighed nothing.

"You know him?"

"I've studied him."

"Who is he?"

"He's Badawi's right hand."

That couldn't be right. "He was going to blow himself up at Sacré-Couer."

"No. He wasn't."

I stretched my neck past his arm and looked down the steps. If Sayed was following us, the rain hid him well.

"Then what was he doing there?"

"He was there to make sure that his people did what they were supposed to do." He made a harsh sound in the back of his throat. "He can't have suicide bombers losing their nerve."

I thought of the boy I'd knocked out.

"Was that a movement behind us?"

"He's back there," I whispered.

"I'm going to put you down." He bent, settling me gently on a step.

Bang!

"*Ooomph.*" My rescuer lurched. His hand clutched the side of his leg and blood welled between his fingers.

I lifted the Glock and spotted a shape in the darkness. I pulled the trigger.

Bang!

Did I get him?

I shot again.

The shape fell straight backward.

For a few long seconds I didn't breathe. I didn't move. I didn't want to. I'd killed another human being.

At least I hoped I had. My hand—the hand holding the Glock—didn't move. I was ready for Sayed to rise up like Glenn Close out of that bathtub in *Fatal Attraction*. "How badly are you hurt?"

"Just a graze." He rested his hand on top of mine and helped me lower the gun. "Nice shot."

I looked up at the guy who'd rescued me. I tried to make out his features, but the rain and his sodden hoodie hid his face.

"It's never easy—" the man's blood was soaking his pant leg "—killing someone."

Tears mixed with the rain on my face and my throat swelled shut. I couldn't speak.

"And it's not supposed to be." He lurched up the next step. "They'll find you here."

"What? You're going?"

He nodded, clapped one hand against his bleeding leg, grabbed the railing with the other, and climbed two more steps.

"Wait! Is it you?"

He stiffened and went no farther. "What do you mean?"

"Are you the guy on the motorcycle? The one who's already saved me twice?"

His shoulders relaxed. "About that?"

"What?"

"Tell the people you're working for that you need more training." He hauled himself up another step.

"Wait!"

"What?" Now he sounded annoyed.

"Thank you."

"No need."

"There is totally a need to thank you."

He stopped again. "You want to thank me?"

"Of course I want to thank you."

"That guy—Jake."

"What about him?" How did he know about Jake?

"Cut him some slack."

I stared. Was it Jake hiding behind the hoodie? If so, he was doing a bang-up job disguising his voice—and build.

"Why do you care about me and Jake?"

"I don't. He's not good enough for you. But when he lied, he did it to protect you."

I squinted through the rain. Who was this guy? "He could have told me the truth."

"Sometimes the truth isn't an option."

What was that supposed to mean?

"Also, it might be better if you didn't mention me." He climbed another few steps.

"Wait!"

This time he didn't stop. He reached the top of the steps and disappeared.

"Poppy!" Chariss's voice cut through the steady rain.

"Here," I called. "I'm here."

Then she was kneeling next to me.

Jake stood behind her. "You're not hurt?" His voice was tight.

"No. I'll be fine."

He staggered. Fell-to-his-knees staggered. "Thank God."

I was feeling fairly staggered myself, but since I was already on the ground, I just lowered my head to the nearest step.

TWENTY-ONE

I stretched out on the velvet couch nearest the fireplace and sighed a contented sigh.

I was warm. I was dry. My ankle was taped. No one whom I cared about had died. Consuela was snuggled next to me. And Chariss hadn't kicked me out of her suite. Life was good.

Jean Fortier sat in the chair closest to the fireplace and looked down at the rumpled newspaper on the glass-topped wheat sheaf table. Above the fold, there were articles about the bombing at Gare du Nord and Pompidou. Below the fold, there was an article about how American actress Chariss Carlton had saved a group of children at Sacré-Couer, then run after one of the terrorists. While lives had been lost, the plan to blow up the beloved basilica had failed.

There was no mention of attacks on Les Deux Magots or the Eiffel Tower.

"What happened at the café?" I asked.

"They had weaponized drones. We got lucky. It was raining too hard for them to fly."

"And at the Eiffel Tower?"

"There were explosives hidden on some of the structural beams."

"How is that even possible?"

Jean's face hardened. "We're figuring that out. The terrorists had inside help. It is most fortunate you killed the man with the detonator code."

I winced. The thought of killing people—even a man like Sayed Hamadei—rubbed against my conscience. "I still don't understand why Ghislain Lambert would be mixed up in all this."

Jean closed his eyes as if the thought of a Frenchman's involvement pained him. "We searched his computer."

"And?"

"There was a private gateway to a dark site—"

"What does that mean?"

"Someone had set up a dummy page. It looked like Galeries Lafayette. If a user put the correct items in the shopping cart, they were taken to another site."

"A terrorist site?"

"Not exactly. The site belonged to men who'd do anything to return France to the way they believe it should be. Lambert helped the terrorists plan these awful things because he believed if the attacks were bad enough, French citizens would rise up and expel the Muslims from our borders."

I pictured the Eiffel Tower tumbling into the Seine. "He thought killing thousands of people was justified?"

"Apparently."

"But it was actual terrorists doing the bombing?"

"Yes. As far as our analysts can tell, the terrorists believed they were dealing with a corrupt banker. They had no idea of Lambert's plan. They believed they were striking a blow for Allah."

I thought about that for a moment.

"We found his body."

"You what?" I sat up straight.

"We found his body in the back of one of the vans the terrorists were using." Jean winced. "He died badly."

More information than I needed. I looked up at the ceiling, where an ornate crystal chandelier hung from a raised medallion. "Would Ghislain's prediction have come true? Would France have expelled its Muslim population?"

Jean answered me with a Gallic shrug. "Let us hope not."

Tap, tap.

"Would you mind answering that?" I waved toward my ankle, which balanced atop three pillows.

"Of course." Jean stood and crossed to the door.

Consuela lifted her head and growled. Deeply.

Given Consuela's warning, I wasn't exactly surprised when John Brown entered the suite. I was surprised to see him carrying Fendi shopping bags.

"Fortier." Mr. Brown transferred the bags to his left hand, extended his right, and waited for the Frenchman to take it.

"Brown."

They shook and stared at each other, mutual distrust sparking between them.

After a few long seconds, Jean turned to me. "I will take my leave. Let me know if you need anything. France is forever in your debt."

When the door closed behind Jean, Mr. Brown took his chair. He put the bags down near me.

Consuela pushed onto her paws and showed her teeth.

"Your dog doesn't like me."

"No," I agreed. "She doesn't."

"I brought your shopping."

The Peekaboo and the trench. I'd forgotten about them. "Thank you."

"We've got a line on another banker."

"*Grrr.*" Consuela did not approve.

"I need more training before you send me out again."

"Maybe." He rubbed his chin. "But part of your value is

that no one would believe you're an agent. If you're too well-trained, that value is gone."

"My lack of training puts the people working with me at risk."

He waved his hand. "Stone is going to be fine."

I knew that. I'd already spoken with Thor. He was convalescing in a bed somewhere deep inside the American embassy.

"In fact—" Mr. Brown made sure he had my full attention "—we've decided the two of you work well together. He's your new partner. We're developing a legend for him now."

"A legend?"

"A fabricated identity."

"I still need training."

MR. BROWN CROSSED his left ankle over his right knee and leaned forward "We didn't ask you to protect French monuments. We asked you to get account numbers. You had plenty of training for that."

"Really?" To date I'd received zero training from the agency.

"All you needed was your smile."

The fur on Consuela's back rose. "*Grrrr.*"

"Consuela disagrees."

"Well—" he leaned back in his chair "—I'm not about to take advice from a dog."

I looked past him and stared at the wall covered with gilt-framed pictures of Coco Chanel. "You know me well enough to know I want to make a difference. Know this. I won't put other agents at risk because you didn't want to take the time to train me."

"What do you mean?"

"Get me training or I'm out."

Mr. Brown's eyes narrowed. He didn't appreciate the new, more forceful me.

"As I see it—" I smiled sweetly "—there are very few women who can get you the kind of access I can. It's a lot easier to train me than it is to find someone who can get herself inside any door anywhere in the world." I thought for a moment. "Except Mexico. I have a feeling doors might be closed to me there. What with Diaz wanting me dead."

"He does want that. Although—"

"Although what?"

"Now that you've told Badawi who was behind his nephew's death, Diaz may have his hands full staying alive himself."

I allowed myself a small smile. "Now that his questions are answered, Badawi won't be trying to have me kidnapped anymore."

"Which is a good thing—" Mr. Brown leaned forward "—because—"

"First training." I wasn't taking *no* for an answer and I wasn't going to let Mr. Brown intimidate me. Not anymore.

"Fine. Training first. You start as soon as the ankle is healed." He stood and a bland smile lit his face. "Remember. You asked for it."

"I'll remember."

He took a few steps toward the door.

I couldn't let him leave. Not till I had an answer. "I have a question."

"Yes?"

"The man on the motorcycle, the one who saved Mark and me. Who is he?"

He tilted his head. Slightly. Like a curious robin. "What makes you think I know?"

"You seem to know most things."

"Not that." He looked me straight in the eye. He didn't

blink. His face was unreadable. So why was I sure he was lying?

"I'll make a deal with you."

His brows rose

"The day I get you the Sinaloan account information is the day you tell me what you know about him."

His lips quirked. "I'll consider it."

"We're here!" Mia burst through the door with André a step behind her. "We're here and we brought you—" she spotted Mr. Brown and stopped dead in her tracks "—I didn't realize you had company."

"Mia, André, this is Mr. Brown from the embassy. He had a few questions about what happened in Montmartre. He was just leaving."

Mr. Brown inclined his chin. "Thank you for your help, Ms. Fields. If we have any other questions, we'll be in touch." He slipped through the door.

"What—" Mia pointed at the Fendi bags "—are those?"

"Jean brought them by. There's a pop-up near his office and I forget them there."

"You forgot new goodies from Fendi?" She dug into one of the bags and pulled out the Peekaboo, holding it up by its handle. "Pretty." She stroked the leather.

"I have something for you." André pulled a shopping bag out from behind his back—an orange bag with brown handles.

"What's that?"

"Chariss and I went to Hermès. She's like the queen of Paris now. I mean it. Parisians think she walks on water. If there are any impossible reservations you've been wanting, now's the time to have Chariss call for them. She can get you in immediately."

Mia poked him.

"Oh. Right." He rubbed his arm where Mia had poked him. "We took that poor Toolbox back to Hermès and

Chariss told the manager you helped save all those people at Sacré-Couer. He gave you a new one." André pulled a new bag from the tissue, this one unmarked by rain or grass or blood.

"Thank you."

He put the bag in my hands. "Look inside."

I opened the handbag and found two neatly folded carrés. "What are these for?"

"Those are from me."

I looked up at him. "Why?"

A flush colored his cheeks. "Dylan sold you out."

"What do you mean?"

"The night you couldn't come to the catacombs. She told someone she thought was a paparazzo where you'd be."

I opened the first scarf. The pattern looked as if it had been painted by Raol Dufy. "Thank you. I love it." I rubbed the rich silk against my cheek. "It's beautiful."

He sat in the chair closest to me, reached forward, and scratched behind Consuela's ears.

She sighed and lowered herself to sitting.

André looked deep into my eyes. "I really am sorry."

"Don't give it another thought."

"So—" Mia took the chair Mr. Brown had vacated "—I have something for you, too." She reached into the giant Louis Vuitton tote she'd dropped at her feet and pulled out a Ladurée box.

"Thank you." I returned the scarf to the bag, carefully placed the bag on the floor next to me, and held my hands out. "You two are the best."

"We know you love macarons."

"And I haven't eaten a single one since I arrived." I opened the box, dithered between salted caramel and vanilla, picked vanilla, and deposited the box on the table next to the newspaper. "Please. Eat some."

André nabbed a pistachio and a chocolate.

Mia went for an orange blossom. She popped it in her mouth and chewed. "So, Chariss saved all those people."

"Uh-huh." I eyed the box on the table. A caramel next?

"Yeah, right. You're really going to let her take all the credit?"

"She deserves all the credit."

"Oh, please. If you want the paparazzi off your back, I get it. But, among the three of us, let's be honest."

"It's better this way. I don't like the spotlight."

"You're sure?"

"Positive." And I was. Chariss was welcome to every single photographer, every single request for interview, and every single headline.

"Where is she?" asked Mia.

"She met Yurgi for a drink."

"Yurgi?"

"Long story. I think she's finally met a man who's a match for her."

Mia's brows rose to her hairline. André's too.

Consuela licked my fingers.

"She's easier to live with when she's in love."

André snagged a lemon macaron.

"So—" Mia stretched out her legs "—are you going to tell us what happened?"

"Yeah." André swallowed the whole macaron. "You knew about the attack before it happened. You made me promise not to go to Sacré-Couer."

Guns and violence and death seemed so far removed from this suite. I ran my hand down Consuela's back. "I found a list at Ghislain's and worried it might be targets. I shared it with French authorities—" I looked at Mia "—you met Jean." Now I looked at André. "I was terrified when you told me you were going to Sacré-Couer."

"You still went."

"I had to. Chariss was there."

As if on cue, Chariss breezed into the suite. She was dressed in cream (head to toe) as if she were some monochromatic angel. "You're awake."

André stood.

Chariss waved at him. "Sit down. You make me feel old."

Consuela rolled her eyes.

"Yurgi sends his regards," she trilled. Then she spotted the macarons and descended like a hungry vulture. "Are there any rose petal? No? How about raspberry?" She bit into a berry macaron and groaned.

"Mia—" André jerked his head toward the door "—we've got that thing."

"We do? Oh. Right. We've got a thing. Poppy, I'll call you later."

A second later they were gone.

"How's Yurgi?" I asked.

"I told him the truth."

"About?"

"About what happened. I couldn't start a relationship with him thinking I was some kind of hero."

She'd told the truth? "You got me up those stairs."

"I've been meaning to ask you about that."

"About what?"

"When I left you, we were midway. When I got back, you were almost to the top."

"I crawled."

"A hundred steps?"

I didn't know why I didn't want to tell her about the man who'd rescued me. It wasn't as if he'd sworn me to secrecy. But keeping him to myself seemed like the right thing to do. "It wasn't easy. Have you seen the bruises on my knees?" Bruises I'd acquired being knocked down by two explosions.

"And while you were crawling up the steps you shot that awful man?" Chariss didn't believe me.

"Exactly."

She stared at me, daring me to continue the lie.

I stared back. "That's what happened."

"One of the people who brought you back here said you shot him right between the eyes."

"I'm just glad I hit him."

"Me, too." She helped herself to another macaron. "Yurgi wants to take us out to dinner."

"Chariss—"

"Before you say no, he just wants to take us to L'Espadon. You don't even have to leave the hotel."

"Fine."

"Fine?"

I had to eat and I didn't feel like arguing. "I like Yurgi."

"You do? You never like the men I date."

"I like him."

She grinned. "Do you want to bring Mark along?"

"He's still on bed rest."

"I stopped by to see him."

"You did?"

"Don't sound surprised. The man got stabbed trying to help me." She held her hand above the box of macarons. "How many calories are in these things?"

"No idea. You saw Mark? He's okay?"

"He'll be fine." She picked another raspberry macaron out the box. "You could do worse."

"What do you mean?"

"I mean he's gorgeous and brave and he obviously has a thing for you."

"A thing?"

"A thing." She nibbled on the edge of her macaron. "You should consider asking him out."

I simply stared.

"Although Viktor will be there tonight, so perhaps it's for the best to wait on Mark."

That wasn't worth a response.

With her free hand, she pulled her phone out of her pocket and looked at the time. "I still have time to get a new dress. Do you mind if I leave you?"

Not at all. "Of course not."

She dropped a kiss on my head, fed Consuela a stray crumb of macaron, and floated out of the suite.

I wrapped an arm around Consuela.

"*Yip.*" She licked my nose.

"I'm glad to be here, too."

Tap, tap.

There was no one available to open the door.

I slid my hand between the sofa cushions and closed my fingers around the grip of the gun I had not yet returned to Mr. Brown. "It's open."

Jake stepped inside. Thunder darkened his golden features. "I can't believe you left the door unlocked. What if I'd been one of Diaz's hitmen?"

I pulled the Glock free of the cushions. "I would have shot you."

"Oh."

"*Yip, yip, yip.*" Consuela was snickering.

"How are you feeling?"

"Tired." I shoved the Glock back between the cushions.

"I thought I'd keep you company." He took the popular chair. The one that faced me directly.

"What do you want, Jake?"

"We should talk."

Ugh. "About what?"

He rested his elbows on his knees and leaned forward. "You said you wanted to make a difference."

"I did say that."

"And you've done it. You saved hundreds of people."

I waited for him to say more.

He didn't.

"*Grrr.*"

I stroked Consuela's fur and stared at him. "Are you saying my mission is accomplished? I should pack my bags and go back to the beach?"

"I'm saying you've done what you set out to do."

"I'm going to keep doing it."

He scowled at the wheat sheaf table as if it was responsible for all the ills in the world—or at least my stubbornness.

"Why can't you believe in me, Jake? Everyone else does."

"It's not that I don't believe in you. I do. It's that I lo—" He shifted his gaze to the fireplace. "It's that I can't stand the thought of you getting hurt."

"I twisted an ankle."

"You went up against one of the most dangerous men in the world."

"And I won." Couldn't he just let me savor being alive? "Would you please hand me that box?" I needed another macaron.

"What if you'd lost?" He held out the box.

I selected a pistachio. "I didn't."

"What if?" he insisted.

Then I would have died making a difference. "You want a what if?"

He blinked.

"What if you hadn't faked your own death? Where would we be now? What if you'd been honest with me?"

"I lied to keep you safe."

I'd heard that before. "Maybe you should give up on protecting me. If you'd believed in me, we'd still be together. We'd have fallen the rest of the way in—" I stopped. I couldn't say the word.

"Are you ever going to forgive me?"

I'd promised the man on the stairs I'd cut Jake some slack, but promising and doing were very different. I'd loved him and he'd lied. I closed my eyes. I'd held my anger close because its fire was easier to handle than the gray weight of sorrow. "Maybe someday."

"Will you consider walking away from Mr. Brown and the agency?"

"Do you want me to forgive you or not?"

"*Grrr.*" Consuela voted no.

"It's dangerous."

"Look, Jake. I saved people. I made a difference. If you think I'm walking away from the chance to do that again, you're wrong." I sat up a little straighter. "I can't wait for what comes next."

ALSO BY JULIE MULHERN

The Poppy Fields Adventures

Fields' Guide to Abduction

Fields' Guide to Assassins

The Country Club Murders

The Deep End

Guaranteed to Bleed

Clouds in My Coffee

Send in the Clowns

Watching the Detectives

Cold as Ice

Shadow Dancing

Back Stabbers

Let's keep in touch!

Send me updates about Julie's books.

Made in the USA
Monee, IL
17 January 2023

25476975R00144